"Sorry," she gasped. "I'm fine, really." She took a deep breath before continuing. "It's catching up. That's all. I keep seeing the road racing at me before you grabbed me."

"The same pictures flashing before ███ ███ le was staring down at her, his eyes ███

All laughter vanished. Repla███ ███ ██ to replace that vision of t███ ███ ███ warmer, kinder, pain-f███ ███ s hands still holding ███ ███ her breathing slowing. ███ ███ u.

"Shh." His mouth was o███ ███ handing and giving. Generous and selfi███

Stretching upward, she slid her arms around his neck and held on to him as though he could save her from the frightening images in her head. She wanted to obliterate the images of the accident from her mind. Jerking back, she dropped her arms to her sides. "Sorry."

The elevator rattled and shook, bumping to a halt.

The door squeaked open.

Lachlan loosened his grip on her. "Tilda?"

Dear Reader,

When plastic surgeon Lachlan McRae overhears a man berating his wife for smashing his beloved car and not asking how she was after a major surgery, he has no idea his colleague's patient is going to tip his heart upside down when they meet up in Cambodia a year later.

Matilda Simmons only wants to get away from home and distract herself from a life that's gone belly-up. Now single—and relieved to be—she wants to find her feet and get on with living life to the fullest. But when she walks out of the airport at Phnom Penh, she doesn't realize just how much her life is about to change.

Can she trust herself to believe in a man again? Can Lachlan move on from the loss of his beloved wife to start over with this amazing woman? Is there happiness waiting for both of them?

Follow these two as they trip their way through their demons to find love. No one makes it easy for them, but love will win out in the end. Just how, is for you to find out as you read their story.

Happy reading,

Sue MacKay

suemackayauthor@gmail.com

FAKE FIANCÉE
TO FOREVER?

SUE MACKAY

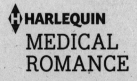

H HARLEQUIN®
MEDICAL
ROMANCE™

Recycling programs
for this product may
not exist in your area.

ISBN-13: 978-1-335-73797-7

Fake Fiancée to Forever?

Copyright © 2023 by Sue MacKay

Harlequin Enterprises ULC
22 Adelaide St. West, 41st Floor
Toronto, Ontario M5H 4E3, Canada
www.Harlequin.com

Printed in U.S.A.

Sue MacKay lives with her husband in New Zealand's beautiful Marlborough Sounds, with the water on her doorstep and the birds and the trees at her back door. It is the perfect setting to indulge her passions of entertaining friends by cooking them sumptuous meals, drinking fabulous wine, going for hill walks or kayaking around the bay—and, of course, writing stories.

Books by Sue MacKay

Harlequin Medical Romance

Queenstown Search & Rescue

Captivated by Her Runaway Doc
A Single Dad to Rescue Her
From Best Friend to I Do?

The GP's Secret Baby Wish
Their Second Chance in ER
Fling with Her Long-Lost Surgeon
Stranded with the Paramedic
Single Mom's New Year Wish
Brought Together by a Pup

Visit the Author Profile page
at Harlequin.com for more titles.

I dedicate this book to my special group of friends
that go on wonderful trips away together.
You ladies rock.

PROLOGUE

TILDA SIMMONS BLINKED. A bright light shone on her eyes. 'Go away,' she muttered.

'Hello, Matilda. I'm Toby, a nurse. You've been in an accident.'

Her head was throbbing something awful. 'I remember. I think.' Hadn't she lost control of the car on black ice while driving to work? Slammed into a brick wall or something?

'You've been sleeping since coming up from Recovery to the general ward after having surgery to your face. The surgeon will explain everything as soon as he's free.'

Hence the headache. 'Thanks.' The nurse wouldn't give her the details. Not his job.

Toby continued. 'Tell me the pain level in your head.'

One to ten, with ten being the worst. 'Six.'

He raised an eyebrow in disbelief, but only said, 'I've got strong analgesics here that the plastic surgeon insists you're to take now you're on the ward.'

In other words, this nurse would make sure she swallowed them, and didn't ignore them.

'I understand. To be honest, I'm happy to have the relief. I feel woozy.' The after-effects of anaesthesia were clouding her mind a little. A new state for her, but as a theatre nurse she'd seen it happen more often than she could recall.

'Glad to hear it.'

Hang on. 'Did you say plastic surgeon?' That meant tissue damage and scarring. On her head? Her face? 'What happened? Am I all right?' Was she going to look like something that scared the pants off little kids? A breath stuck in her throat. She sucked in hard, coughed out, aggravating her tender throat. Breathed in again, ignoring the increased pounding behind her eyes.

'Easy.' Toby touched her upper arm. 'Everything's going to be fine. You've been lucky. The wound is on the side of your face by the hairline. Not to mention your surgeon is one of the best.' He was watching her closely, no doubt keeping an eye on her vital signs. 'You're in Western General Hospital, by the way.'

'What's wrong with me?' Panic struck. She

was a nurse, so she should know what was going on. Shouldn't she?

Again the nurse's firm hand pressed her upper arm. 'Steady. You've had a knock to the head. This is a normal reaction to shock and surgery.'

True. She nodded and pain stabbed behind her eyes. 'Can you break the rules and tell me what my injuries are?' For the life of her, she couldn't remember what she'd been told before being carted off to Theatre. Probably nothing too detailed at that point, if she was even conscious.

'Think this is where I come in.' A man stepped around the nurse. 'I'm Gary Cook, your plastic surgeon today.' Standing beside the narrow bed, he continued. 'It appears that your head hit the steering wheel and the side of your left cheek split wide open. I've put everything back together with layers of suturing. Your forehead also needed stitching. Your left clavicle's fractured but according to the orthopaedic surgeon who read your X-ray earlier you don't need surgery for that. Time and rest will take care of it. From your GCS I'd say you've got severe concussion so no partying for a few weeks.'

Fat chance of that even if she wasn't in here. James didn't like her going out and enjoying herself with friends. So her Glasgow Coma Score had been low. 'How low?'

'Four. But it's normal now. You came through surgery without a hitch. From here on it's all about getting better. I'm recommending you stay in hospital for at least two nights, but we'll monitor you before that's a definite.'

Right now this was all too much to take in.

'Thank you.' Her eyes were closing of their own volition and she couldn't find the energy to raise her eyelids again. She'd prefer to do without the after-effects from surgery, but it seemed she'd stuffed up driving and this was the price. An image of racing towards a brick wall filled her head. Something like a groan fell over her lips. It could've been a lot worse. A hell of a lot worse.

'You're safe, Matilda.' The nurse touched her hand.

The next thing she was aware of was waking again with a monitor beeping somewhere behind her head.

Toby had a blood pressure cuff around her arm. 'Welcome back, Matilda.'

'Hi,' Tilda managed. From now on she'd try not to be so damned cheery with her patients. It seemed a bit OTT while lying here feeling utterly useless.

'One to ten, with ten the worst, what's the pain level in your head?'

Twelve. 'Seven.'

'I'll talk to the duty surgeon and see if we can give you something stronger for that. In the meantime, do you want a drink of water?'

Her mouth was a desert. 'Please.'

'I'll go get it. I'll also tell your husband he can come in. He's pacing the floor of the waiting room, desperate to see you. He's not happy we wouldn't let him in until you woke up, but as you'll know sleep's the most important thing for you right now.'

James was here? When he'd been heading to Banff for business? When he'd left in a foul mood because she hadn't picked up his dry-cleaning yesterday?

'How long ago did I crash?'

'Roughly four hours.'

So James had turned around to come back and see her. After the massive argument they'd had she half expected him to have stayed away on purpose. Her heart softened. They mightn't agree on much these days but he had returned home to see her. Something was going right.

'You wrecked my car.' James stood at the end of the bed, glaring at her. 'It's ruined. After all the hard work I put in to get it up to speed and looking the best on the road, you go and drive it into a wall.'

Forget it. They weren't getting on. Why had she thought they might? Those days were long gone.

'It was an accident, James,' she said wearily. 'I struck black ice.' Nothing wrong with her memory after all—unfortunately.

'So what? If you can't handle a powerful car then you shouldn't have been driving. Don't you even care about what you've done?'

Didn't he care about her and if she was going to be all right?

'I am sorry.' She truly was because he loved that car, but she'd also like some recognition as his wife, who he was also supposed to love. She wasn't just some woman who'd crashed his favourite vehicle.

'Sorry?' he yelled. 'You think that makes everything all right? You stupid woman. Sorry doesn't begin to cover it.'

'Go away, James. I don't need this right now.' Proof that he really didn't love her enough. Not enough to be worried after a serious accident had landed her in hospital anyway. 'Go.'

Lachlan couldn't believe what he was hearing from the room where a woman was recovering from surgery. What sort of man would tear strips off his wife in that situation? Or at any time. Not once had the guy asked how she was feeling. He hadn't shown even a hint of concern. To Lachlan, it seemed to be all about the car.

Leaping up from the desk, he strode across to the room where the woman lay looking upset. Along with tired and defeated. Quite a sorry picture. 'Excuse me, Mr Simmons?'

'Who wants to know?'

'James, quieten down, will you?' Matilda Simmons gasped.

Lachlan intervened before the guy started ranting again. 'I'm Lachlan McRae, another plastic surgeon on the ward,' he told the distressed woman. 'I couldn't help overhearing your husband.' The whole ward probably had.

'James' surname is Connell, not Simmons.'

'Mr Connell, your wife's had serious surgery this morning. She needs to rest.' He paused, waiting for the guy to ask how she was and how the op had gone.

'Hope you knew what you were doing. Her face looks terrible.'

For the first time in his career, Lachlan wanted to plant his fist in someone's face—this man's in particular, so he'd feel the pain his wife was dealing with. It took a long, deep breath to keep his anger at bay.

'I didn't perform the procedure but I know there'll be scarring for some time to come, but long-term Matilda will barely see where she's been injured.' Yes, he did add emphasis to 'injured' because someone had to get through to this man that his wife had been seriously wounded.

'Think you could put my car back together in the same condition it was when I left home this morning?' Connell was yelling again, glaring at his wife.

She winced, embarrassment now the most obvious emotion on her bruised face. 'James, shut up,' she whispered.

'What? You don't want people knowing what an idiot you've been?'

Lachlan watched the patient roll carefully onto her side, her back to her husband, and he said, 'Mr Connell, I have to ask you to leave now. Your wife needs to rest,' he repeated a little louder than before.

'I'll stay as long as I want,' the man shouted. Was this his only way of making a point? To shout so loudly everyone within a hundred metres heard?

'Please stop yelling. There are other patients in need of quiet. This is a hospital. People are here because they're unwell. We do not tolerate behaviour like yours, Mr Connell.' Now *he* was raving. His anger was unusual. Something about his patient's vulnerability had him wanting to protect her from more than a damaged face. 'I am advising you to go. Now.'

'Need a hand in here?' Toby stood in the doorway. A large man with shoulders like a brick wall, he could make people quiver with a stare should he feel the need. He was also the gentlest nurse on the surgical ward.

'I think we're fine. Mr Connell was just leaving.'

Absolute silence fell. All eyes were on the husband. Even Matilda had turned just enough to see what her husband did. She appeared to be holding her breath.

'See you later.' The man stomped out of the room as Toby stepped aside.

Lachlan's chest rose and fell normally and the tension in his gut eased. 'Thanks, Toby.'

'You had it under control.' The nurse came into the room, speaking softly. 'Matilda, I'm back to harass you. How're you feeling? Pain level?'

'Five,' she uttered. 'I'm good. Truly. I'm a nurse and know about these things.'

'Where do you work?' Lachlan asked. He didn't recognise her, but then her face was swollen and bruised.

'I'm a theatre nurse at St Michael's, Gastown.'

'That'll be why we haven't come across each other then. I don't do ops there.'

'It's a good crew there.' She was fading. Everything catching up with her once more?

'Anything I can get you?' he asked, wanting to help any way he could.

'My phone?'

Toby spoke up. 'If it's in your bag which is on the bedside table then you're in luck. The paramedic found it in the car and brought it in with you.'

Lachlan stepped closer. 'Like me to pass you the bag?' He didn't want her moving any more than necessary. *And* he wanted to offer her a hand getting what she required. Which at the moment didn't include a ranting husband. Instead she needed to relax and sleep off the shock resulting from the accident.

'Can you get my phone out?' She managed a wobbly smile. 'There's nothing in there that'll bite, I promise.'

Her smile nudged him on the inside. Which shouldn't happen. This woman was a patient, no more, no less. But he was still angry at the way her husband had treated her so could be he was being a little soft.

'Good to know, since I need my fingers

for work.' Delving into a woman's handbag seemed a bit like stepping onto a minefield. Not that he'd ever done that, but when he'd worked in the States he'd put a soldier's hand back together who had, and triggered a small bomb as he did so. 'Here you go.'

He handed the phone to Matilda before stepping out of the room, where he sucked in a lungful, then let it go. No one should be abused by a loved one. The way Connell spoke to his wife was appalling. While she was still recovering from surgery and shock, at that. He leaned against the wall, eyes closed, and breathed out his bad mood. Time to move on. The woman's relationship woes were not his problem.

Suddenly he was thinking of Kelly, his late wife. Not once had he spoken to her like Connell had to Matilda. The man should be holding onto his wife for dear life. He had no idea how lucky he was she'd survived. Four years ago when a driver fell asleep at the wheel of his car and drove into Kelly, she'd died instantly. *His* arms had felt empty ever since. An emptiness he doubted would ever be filled again.

'Janet? It's me, Tilda.'

Lachlan straightened at the sound of the distressed voice coming from the room behind him.

'I'm in hospital. I had an accident on the way to work.' Pause. 'I'm all right. Promise.' Pause. 'Because I had surgery on my face.' A longer pause. When she spoke next her voice was full of tears. 'I can't take any more, Janet. I've tried and tried to be good enough for him.'

Lachlan hissed air over his bottom teeth. Love had been easy for him and Kelly. From day one, they'd had each other's backs and both their plans for the future and their hearts had been completely in sync.

In the room behind him Matilda was getting worked up. 'When I get out of here, can I stay with you for a while? Just until I find my own place. I'm done with James.'

Lachlan walked away before he heard any more. Matilda Simmons seemed to be moving on from her marriage, but that might only be temporary. She had yet to get over what had happened earlier in the day, and right now her mind would be all over the place. Whatever she did, it was none of his business.

CHAPTER ONE

Twelve months later

HER PACK SLUNG on her back, Tilda stepped through the main doors into the arrivals hall at Phnom Penh Airport and looked for a man holding a card with her name on it. She presumed that was how he intended getting her attention. Or would he rely on memory? If he even recognised her name. It'd been a surprise to read who'd be meeting her at the airport. Showed just how small the world could be. And how her mind hadn't been a complete blank at the time, because she was sure she'd recognise him.

Matilda Simmons.

She checked out the relaxed man holding the piece of card and laughed. Mr Lachlan McRae, plastic surgeon, hadn't changed a bit since she'd last seen him on the ward where she'd recuperated from the accident that changed her life for ever. He mightn't have been her surgeon but he'd been in and out of the room she'd shared with a patient of his. She hadn't imagined the good looks. That face was chiselled and now sported a light stubble that was even more attractive. Sexy came to mind. She shoved that thought away fast. She was done with men except for the occasional one-night stand just to remind herself she still had some appeal to the male species. James had killed her need to be loved.

Growing up with only her grandmother, she'd always longed for more family and thought she was on the way to finding it when she and James fell in love. Turned out his idea of loving was telling her how to live her life in a way that suited him. She'd believed in him, loved him to bits, and that was how he'd repaid her. If that was what men wanted from her then from here on out she was going solo. Even once the divorce became final she wouldn't be rushing out to find a man to give her heart to.

That included this particular man, who was smiling as though he did recognise her. Might just be his friendly nature. She'd looked different back then, with her face red and tight around the glaring scars. These days her hair was longer and hung loose to cover the worst of those, though they had already faded some, as Mr Cook had assured her they would.

Crossing over, she held out her hand. 'Hello, Lachlan. Funny how we've ended up working for the same charity at the same time.'

'Hi, Matilda.' He shook her hand, his fingers warm to the touch. Or was that because she felt tired and a little chilly after the long flight, despite the humid air here? 'I did get a surprise when your name came up on the list. A nice one, I have to say.' That made her feel warmer but no more interested, other than as a colleague. He continued, 'I'm meant to pick up another guy as well, but his flight's been delayed and he won't be here until tomorrow morning.'

'So we're going out to the medical centre now?' From what she'd read online it might be about an hour away, and right now she'd really had enough of sitting in one seat for any length of time. A shower and a walk would be preferable, except she understood that wasn't happening until she got to the Hospital Care Charity's staff quarters.

'Can I carry your pack for you?'

There were a few too many clothes and shoes inside, plus some books to read when she wasn't on duty or out sightseeing, but that was her problem.

'I'm good, thanks.'

'Okay. Over here.' He led the way outside. 'In answer to your question, we're staying in town overnight. I hope that's all right with you? There're no surgeries scheduled for to-morrow morning so Harry, he's the administrator, suggested that since I have to be at the airport first thing to pick up Dave we might as well stay at a hotel in the city. It'll make it easier for you to unwind and get a decent night's sleep as it's kind of noisy where our quarters are, right next to the clinic on a main road. I say let's make the most of the opportunity.'

Seemed someone was looking out for her.

'Perfect.'

'Harry booked us rooms at a small hotel one street back from the Mekong River. I wondered if you'd like to take a walk and maybe have a meal so that you can stay up to a reasonable hour and get your body clock on track for normal as soon as possible.'

It came back in a rush. This man's deep voice, full of kindness when James had been so outrageous. Seemed nothing had changed. Still deep and kind. But there *was* a difference; he had a twinkle in his eyes and a lightness in his face that she hadn't seen then. That was professional. This was friendly. He made her feel welcome in Cambodia when it wasn't up to him to do that.

'That was my plan—stay up until about ten. Not sure if it actually works, but I intend trying.' They'd reached a large parking area and were weaving through slow-moving vehicles of all descriptions. Lachlan seemed focused on both traffic and her. She liked him already. 'How long have you been in Phnom Penh?'

'Three weeks. Two to go. It's a wonderful place. The people are so open and pleasant while busy trying to make ends meet. I've never done anything like this before and I'll definitely volunteer again. What about you?'

'First time too.' Two years ago she'd applied to work for a month at a charity clinic in Laos but James had hated the idea of her going away to help others. He'd said she had no right to leave him alone for a month. In the end she'd capitulated because it made life easier. 'I'm hoping it'll be a great way to meet locals and get to understand their lifestyle a little.'

'You'll get to do that, for certain. Here we are.' Locks pinged on a dented car in front of them. 'The car belongs to the clinic.'

'It's seen better days.' She laughed through a deep yawn. The long-haul flight was catching up with her big time.

'Sure has. Did you get any sleep on the plane?' Lachlan took her pack and stashed it on the back seat.

She couldn't remember him being so intriguing before, but her mind had been on other things. James and his damned car. Anyway, she'd been married then and wouldn't have looked twice at another man. Now she was single and still not looking twice. For different reasons though. Marriage was a total commitment. Running solo meant looking after her heart, and she no longer trusted herself to know when she'd found a good man.

The man beside her seemed more relaxed and casual away from work. It suited him. To get to know him a bit more might be interesting if she was on the lookout for someone to have fun with, but she wasn't. Not even for a one-night stand? Maybe. Despite the heat bouncing off the tarmac she shivered. Where did that idea come from? He was only here for another two weeks. It could work. Or not. Another yawn widened her mouth. But there was no denying her life had been a bit dull lately. Was she only just realising that when there was a hot man beside her?

'I dozed a little. Bit hard when I had a wriggly ten-year-old on one side and a woman on the other who spread out over more than her own seat.' The joys of flying economy class. She'd never flown any other way.

Lachlan winced as he opened the door for her. 'Hate it when that happens. Climb in and we'll head into the city.'

A gentleman. Why wasn't she surprised? She recalled his tact with James when he was berating her for wrecking his favourite car. It had been apparent even in her post-op state that the surgeon hadn't been happy with her husband but he'd remained cool, calm and collected as he should, even though she wasn't his patient. Which was more than she'd been.

She'd cried after James had gone that day, lots of tears of frustration and disappointment. Of course, shock from the accident had added to her distress too, but reality had finally set in. James was never again going to be the loving, kind man she'd fallen for.

The longer they were married, the more selfish he'd become and the more controlling he'd tried to be. It hadn't helped that he'd taken to drinking as a way of drowning his woes, the biggest of which was apparently her. He'd been furious when she'd learned she was pregnant. That was not in his plans. He'd demanded she get an abortion. She'd refused, which had really rocked the boat as she was not meant to go against his demands. He didn't like it when she stood up to him. Which hadn't been often enough, she reflected grimly. But when it came to the baby, she'd refused to give in. Except, in the end, he'd won in a roundabout way. She'd miscarried at eleven weeks, and to this day still missed her baby and all the promise that would've come with him or her. She'd never hurt her child, before or after it was born.

Her mother had died from a haemorrhage giving birth to her, and her grandmother had told her often how much she'd wanted to be a mother even though the father had refused to acknowledge the pregnancy. To the point that he'd threatened to hurt her mother if she'd tried to stay in touch.

'Where are you? Not nodding off, are you?' Lachlan's deep voice cut into her thoughts.

'Not at all.' Looking out at the chaos that was the traffic, she asked, 'What's it like driving here?' There was lots of tooting as drivers dodged around other vehicles. Add in tuk-tuks ducking and dodging amongst the faster vehicles and it was bedlam.

Lachlan tossed her a wry grin. 'I won't talk a lot for the next little while. It's kind of crazy, yet I admit I get a thrill out of making it from A to B in one piece.'

'That sounds scary.'

'It's really not that bad, and the speed's fairly slow despite how it looks.'

'Tell me about the clinic. How many people are working there?' Should she be asking him questions when he'd said he wouldn't be talking much? 'Don't answer if you have to concentrate.'

'I can do two things at once, despite being a man and saying I wouldn't talk much. There're ten volunteers at the moment, though that number changes almost weekly. Along with me, there's a general surgeon doing small ops, nothing major. There's one anaesthetist and everyone else is a nurse or paramedic from various countries. You and I are the only Canadians at the moment.' He did talking and driving at the same time very well.

No doubting he *was* a man either. Muscular without being overly so, his strength apparent in his firm body. Throw in good looks and he was quite the package. If she was looking for a guy to get close to—but she wasn't, she chastised herself. Remember James. Usually she never forgot, even for a moment.

'I've been in Toronto for the past ten months. I had another nursing job lined up in Quebec starting two months ago, but the nurse I was replacing changed his mind about leaving. That's when I saw an article about the charity hospital here and how they needed a nurse urgently.'

Her mouth was getting away from her. She wasn't into sharing about herself since she'd walked away from James. Hadn't been inclined to do so before that either. People didn't need to know anything about her other than she was a highly capable nurse. But talking about work had little to do with her private life, so why not be friendly? There was nothing to lose and maybe something enjoyable to gain.

'You moved away from Vancouver after the accident?' He didn't sound too surprised. Did that mean he remembered James ranting about the car?

She'd started this, so she might as well get it out of the way. 'After I left hospital I never returned home. My marriage was over. I stayed with a nursing colleague until I'd fully recovered, then headed east for a change of scenery and to sort out my stuff. Now I'm here in Cambodia.' It was exciting, to say the least.

'What's next for you?'

'I've sent a couple of applications for theatre positions to hospitals back in Canada, but I'm not holding my breath as it's at least a month before I'll be available and most places want an immediate start.'

'My partners and I do most of our work at

Western General and they're always looking for theatre nurses.'

'I'll keep that in mind.' She might've had enough of working with Lachlan by the time he finished up here. Then again, they might well hit it off and she could want to see more of him. At work. Nowhere else. Lachlan might be kind and considerate, and built like a basketballer, but so what? Throw in how she felt more than a little bit hot sitting beside him, and she did feel a slight connection to him, but nothing would come of it.

She was well and truly over James, but the thought of another long-term relationship gave her the shivers. She intended remaining independent from now on. No one was ever again going to tell her how to live her life. Growing up with only her grandmother to share her achievements and failings with, she didn't need a man at her side all the time. Didn't need one, but would love to have some fun, just so long as he wasn't a control freak.

In the beginning James had been so loving and devoted that she'd wondered what she'd done to deserve him. Only after they'd got married did his true colours start to show. He had to be in charge of everything, and expected her to run round after him whenever he demanded. Belittling her grew to be his favourite pastime. Whenever she'd done something he deemed wrong he'd acted like a toddler throwing his toys out of the pram.

His total disregard for her after the accident had been the final blow. Not once had he asked if she was going to be all right. Not once. He had returned to visit her in hospital after his first outburst, but only to give her a full rundown on the damage done to his precious vehicle. His spiel hadn't lasted long. The nurses had overheard—hard not to when he was shouting so loudly—and this time they'd removed him from the ward with the warning not to return. She'd backed them on that. Coming not long after his reaction to her pregnancy and miscarriage, it'd been the last straw. He'd been shocked when she'd walked away from their marriage without a backwards glance, stunned she didn't kowtow to him.

Surprise, James. I am stronger than you gave me credit for.

Something to remember at all times.

Lachlan was still talking. 'Did you enjoy Toronto? I specialised there. It's a massive city.'

'Too big, I reckon. I felt lost without the sea nearby.' Going down to Kitsilano Beach for a swim or a spot of paddleboarding had been one of the highlights of living in Vancouver previously. 'The lake was far too cold for anything but walking along the bank.'

He nodded. 'Vancouver felt almost tropical when I returned home, though that feeling didn't last into winter.'

'I won't have to worry about chilly temperatures for a few weeks.' She'd packed one jacket and a jersey just in case, but doubted they'd ever come out of her bag.

'Here it's the humidity that gets to you. It can be quite draining.'

She could listen to him talking all day. His voice was smooth and had her imagining his fingers moving just as smoothly on her skin. Might be time to get out there and have some short-term fun. Not with Lachlan though. Why not? Um, because...they had to work together? Because... She had no idea, other than a strong instinct to look out for herself and something about this man suggested he could make her feel vulnerable if she wasn't careful. And careful had been her middle name since the day her grandmother had been injured in a freak accident at the amusement park she'd taken Tilda to for her sixth birthday. She'd had to stay in social welfare care for a week as there was no one else to look after her. Since then she'd been careful about getting close to people, afraid they could get taken away from her. Seemed she'd dropped the ball when James came along. That wouldn't happen again. She knew better now. Should've known better the first time.

'Did I mention parking is a pain in the backside?' Lachlan did a loop of the block where the hotel stood.

His passenger laughed, a warm, happy sound, touching him in an unexpected way, making him feel cheerful, and not looking for a hidden agenda. It was more than a relief.

Meredith, a friend he'd known all his life and who'd married his best mate, Matt, had begun playing on his kindness ever since Matt's death eighteen months ago. She'd like Lachlan to move in and become her husband and father to her three boys because it would make life easier for her. He'd told her no. He understood she wanted to have one big happy family so they could move on from the tragedy, but it wouldn't work the way she'd suggested. Anyway, it was her parents and his who were really behind the idea of them getting together, as they'd always hoped he and Meredith would marry one day.

What no one understood was that while losing Matt had rocked him big time, losing Kelly a few years earlier had already broken his heart. He couldn't love again, and while

Meredith claimed that was fine and she'd care for them all, he still could not do what she'd asked. What if someone else died? Him? Where would that leave the little guys then? Up a creek without a paddle didn't begin to come close. Which was why he wasn't getting into a relationship ever again. Losing Kelly had decimated him, and just when he'd finally started getting back on his feet Matt went and dropped dead. Go figure. He clearly could not trust those he loved to stay around for ever.

Someone tapped his arm. Matilda. She said with a cheeky smile, 'Do one of those Italian parking tricks I've seen online where you put the front to the kerb and the back pokes out into the street.'

'It's tempting, but think I'll go with legal and safe.' He didn't want a parking ticket turning up at the clinic after he'd left the country. A hassle no one needed.

'There.' Matilda pointed. 'It'll be a tight squeeze, but we should fit in.'

Was she setting him up for a fail? He loved a challenge, and this one would be a breeze. 'Watch this.' Better not make a mess of it. He didn't. The space was small but so was the car. Driving was one thing he was good at. Along with repairing scars and making patients feel better about themselves.

'Not bad,' she drawled, and shoved open her door. Her dark brown hair fell across her cheek as she turned to smile at him. He ached to reach across and run his fingers through it. Stunned, he gripped the steering wheel hard. Where did that idea come from? It was so not like him. He had to work with Matilda. She'd probably have slapped him if he had reached over and touched her. She should. It would be too intimate an action. He vaguely remembered her hair had barely come below her ears a year ago. He preferred the shoulder-length style she wore now. It suited her better and softened her features.

How had she coped over the intervening time? At least she'd dumped that scumbag. Best thing she could've done. Not every woman had what it took to walk away from a control freak like her husband. The guy had been beyond horrible. That day in the ward, overhearing him raving at Matilda, his protective side had come raging to the fore and had him wanting to intervene. Fortunately his professional side had won out or he might've found himself before the hospital board explaining his behaviour, even when she hadn't been his patient. To his credit, it would've only been a verbal confrontation. He didn't go around hitting people, although his fists had tightened at one point. But there was no denying how much he had wanted to keep his colleague's patient safe, and that had nothing to do with his medical calling.

'You're looking good, a lot more relaxed than you were in hospital.'

Her eyes widened. 'I would hope so.'

Make him feel foolish for mentioning it, why didn't she?

'Moving to Toronto helped, I presume?' He was digging a bigger hole by the minute, but he couldn't help himself. There was so much he wanted to know about Matilda. Which was strange since he didn't like getting involved with people and knowing too much about them, then feeling protective of them. Might be better to remember he'd only add to her problems with his determination to keep his own emotions safe. If she even looked at him twice.

There were already enough people relying on him back home and he'd needed some time out for himself, hence being in Cambodia. The time had come to start living his own life again, only he didn't know exactly where to start. When this opportunity had come up his two partners in the plastic surgery clinic they'd started five years earlier had been blunt in their insistence he take it and have a complete change. They were covering for him back home, which added to his guilt. He'd let them down. Sure, he worked hard but he'd changed from the cheerful specialist to a surgeon who turned up for work just because it was where he was meant to be. After three weeks here he already felt the thrill for his work coming back. No pressure, just doing what he loved. Exactly what he needed and enjoyed.

Getting out of the car, Matilda paused. Looking at him, she nodded. 'I didn't know anyone when I landed in Toronto, yet I fitted in with flatmates and work colleagues easily. That showed me I wasn't incompetent or useless without James to point me in the right direction.'

'Your confidence grew.' He'd have thought she was already confident if she'd left her husband while recovering from a major accident.

'I'd say more like it returned. I got back most of what I'd lost over the years of my marriage. I'm very happy now being single.' Her lips clamped shut as a stunned expression crossed her pretty face. Perhaps she thought she was talking too much? She opened the back door and reached in for her pack.

So she wasn't rushing to find a new life partner. That surprised him. She seemed open and friendly, and he couldn't imagine her being on her own for ever. Though he understood how hard it was to move on after being hurt so badly.

As she slung the pack over her slim shoulders she said, as though speaking to herself, 'I'm dying for a shower.'

He tried to not think about that image. Instead he led the way inside the small hotel and up to the counter. When they'd checked in and had keys in their hands, he asked, 'How about we meet back down here in an hour and go for a walk alongside the Mekong before heading to the Correspondents' Club for a meal?'

'Can we make that half an hour? I'll fall asleep if I have to wait around, and then there'll be no waking me. I do want to stay awake for a few more hours.'

'Dave gave me your phone number in case we missed each other at the airport so I can call you in thirty minutes if you don't show up.' For some inexplicable reason he was pleased to have the number so he could get in touch with her if they weren't both at the clinic at the same time. They might get to spend time together outside the clinic over the next couple of weeks. He'd been sightseeing a few times with other volunteers whenever they had free time, and he'd like to show Matilda the places he'd already seen.

'Thanks.'

'See you shortly,' he said as she headed for the stairs, looking lovely despite the exhaustion coming off her in waves. She wouldn't be running solo long, or without friends. She was *too* lovely not to be popular.

Careful, Lachlan.

'There is an elevator, Matilda.'

Her hand waved at him over her shoulder. 'It's only one floor and I can't wait for that shower. I must stink something awful after so long in the air.'

'Can't say I noticed.' That might be because he'd been too busy keeping an eye on the road as well as Matilda's physical attributes and everything else about her except her aroma. So far, she'd come up trumps in every respect. Unfortunately.

The woman disturbing him paused, one foot on the first stair, and turned to face him. 'It's Tilda, by the way.'

'Right. Tilda.' Not Matilda.

A tired grin split her face. 'See you shortly.'

Kapow. Right in the solar plexus. He felt it like a physical blow. Hard. Swift. Sexy as hell. Nothing to do with the image of her as a naughty child, and all to do with this stunning woman staring at him, blinding him to reality. What reality? The one where he wasn't looking for a partner? Although if he did find one for himself, that might make Meredith wake up to what she was trying to make him do and realise it was never going to work. But that wouldn't be fair on any woman he got even a little bit close to.

'Back here in thirty.' The clock should start ticking now, as right at this moment he needed as long a break from Matilda as possible. *Tilda*. Time to get his breath back and put his sensible head on. Throw the other one away before he got in too deep, wondering what lay behind that friendly façade. He needed to remember the pain when he'd lost Kelly and admit he was not going to be setting himself up for more of that any time soon.

Tilda trudged up the stairs, exhaustion pouring off her in waves. Not a fan of long-haul flights then. But who was? Not him.

He could suggest they take the car to the club but she'd said she needed to walk and get some fresh air. Fresh air. Bring it on. Thirty minutes. He followed her up the stairs, confused and not liking the fact he was getting so stirred up by Tilda.

Coming to Cambodia had given him space to look at his home situation more clearly. When he'd introduced Matt to Meredith at a party they'd instantly fallen for each other. A wedding and three sons later, Matt had died.

A fit, energetic man, his heart had just quit on him at the 10K mark in a local half marathon. Despite all the medical help on hand for the race, nothing could be done to save him. He was gone, leaving everyone devastated. Leaving Meredith and their three young boys for ever. It had been hell. Still was some days. There were times he struggled to accept what had happened.

He'd done everything possible for the boys so they had a male role model to rely on. He adored the little guys. They were awesome. They came and went in his house as they wished. Living just around the corner made it easy for them to pop in and out. Too easy maybe, but no way could he turn them away. Nor could he marry their mother simply for their sakes. He'd never been attracted to Meredith. In the long run that would be a mistake that would affect everyone, and he'd find it almost impossible to come back from.

Up ahead, Tilda turned right along the hallway to her room.

Lachlan turned left. He could already tell she was beautiful inside and out. Who'd have thought a year ago he'd ever think that about another woman? Not him, that was for sure. He didn't usually get side-tracked so easily.

CHAPTER TWO

'I FELL ASLEEP in the shower,' Tilda told Lachlan as they strolled along the riverside. Right after she'd rinsed the conditioner out of her hair she'd leaned against the wall to let the warm water slide over her achy muscles and the next thing she knew she was sliding downwards to land on her butt, water pouring all over her.

Lachlan walked with his hands in his pockets, his shoulders loose, like he had all the time in the world. He probably did tonight. A well-earned break in a hectic schedule?

'Just as well I didn't panic when you were a few minutes late coming downstairs and send someone in to check up on you.'

That would've been interesting.

'They'd have got as big a shock as me,' she said with a laugh. Looking around, she sighed with happiness. The smells of street food wafted past her nose, making her hungry, while the sounds of traffic and people laughing, talking and shouting in languages she didn't understand filled her head. 'This is awesome. To think I'm walking on the bank of the Mekong River. It's an icon for this part of Asia.'

Her companion laughed. 'It's muddy.'

'And very wide. Bet nothing gets in its way.' She pinched herself and looked around at the city behind them. 'I can't believe I'm really here.'

'It's so different to home.'

'Vancouver is your home town?'

'Yes. I did time in different places while qualifying but returned once I was ready to establish my career. My family's there, and my closest friends. I've no desire to move away when everything and everyone I want is nearby.'

'Fair enough.' She'd grown up in Vancouver but had no real attachment to anywhere except the little house in Langley where her grandmother and her mother had also grown up. It had been a sad day when the house had been sold to pay for Grandma's room at a rest home.

'We cross the road here.' Lachlan looked in both directions. 'Any rate, I think we do. We'll give it a go and see what's on the other side.'

'You haven't been to the club before?'

'Once. The first night I arrived in town, Harry picked me up and brought me into the city for a meal before driving us out to the clinic. He seemed glad to get away for a few hours and was in no hurry to return to base. There was no mention of staying over for the night though. He takes his responsibilities very seriously. Quite happy for everyone else to get away for a few hours or more, but rarely does he do the same.'

She was terrified of stepping off the footpath into the crowded road. 'They're all out of control.' There was nothing orderly about where the vehicles went or how close they came to others as they passed with horns blaring non-stop.

He grabbed her hand. 'The rule is once you step off the sidewalk and out into the traffic, don't stop. The drivers will see you and dodge around you, but if you try avoiding them they haven't a clue where you're heading and things can get messy.'

They reached the other side of the road, alive and in one piece.

'See? We made it.' Lachlan was laughing like he'd just had the most exciting experience of his life. If that was the case he needed to get out more often.

With me? she wondered. Might as well since

she was here to have fun as well as help people. Huh? Hadn't she already admonished herself for thinking he was different to other men? As in turn-up-the-heat different.

'What's that building up ahead? Two storeys, big windows, lots of lights.'

'Our destination. Well spotted. Let's get inside and away from all the jabbing elbows.' He let go of her hand.

Despite the loss of connection, Tilda didn't try to put any distance between them. It felt good to be walking alongside him, close but not quite touching. As if they were an item. Obviously they weren't and were not likely ever to be, but she could pretend for a little while. There'd be no consequences when Lachlan wasn't falling over with eagerness to get to know her better.

Being happy walking to a club for a meal with him didn't mean she was giving up her hard-earned independence. The time in Toronto had made her realise she could once more rely on her choices and judgements when it came to where she lived and worked and who she went out with, so long as nobody was looking for anything permanent. She'd become a toughened-up version of the Matilda who'd married James. He'd been her one big mistake and she wasn't willing to make another.

Lachlan opened the door and nodded for her to go first. She quickly scoped him out, felt her eyes widen.

Settle down, Tilda. This is a man you're going to be working with for a couple of weeks. You do not need to create any complications because you're tired after a long flight and excited to be in a new country.

A light hum of voices reached her as they climbed the stairs to the main floor. Mostly Westerners, she realised. Made sense, given the name of the place.

'Is this a public club?'

'Yes. Known for its great food and cold beers.' Lachlan led the way to the bar. 'No Cambodian food. They leave that for the locals and the markets. This is more your burger and pizza stop.'

Her mouth watered. 'I can't wait.'

'Didn't you eat on the plane?' he asked with that mischievous twinkle in his eye. 'Or do you like four meals a day?'

'Since I don't know what day I'm on I'll go with the message from my stomach and eat.' Tomorrow she'd get back to normal, whatever that might be here.

When they left the club an hour later Lachlan texted for a tuk-tuk to take them to their hotel. 'Might as well make the most of the city

by night while we're here. The driver I'm con-
tacting is Kiry, a local man who picks up most
of our patients to bring them to the hospital
and then takes them home when they're ready
to leave. He also hires out his tuk-tuk in the
city at night.'

'Busy man, by the sound of it.'

'Very. Here he is.'

They squeezed into the back, their thighs,
hips and arms pressed against each other.

'Is your child a boy or girl?' Tilda asked
about the small child sound asleep in a safety
seat at the front after Lachlan introduced her.
A tiny screwed-up face was just visible from
its cocoon of blankets.

'Is boy. Phala. My first son.'

'He's lovely. You bring him out with you
every night?'

'My wife works. A cleaner at hospital.
Nights.'

They both worked nights, meaning someone
had to look after their son. It couldn't be easy.

'You're busy people.'

The driver relaxed a little. Because she
hadn't criticised him? 'We are. Have to keep
roof over heads.'

'Show us a little of the city,' Lachlan said
to him.

Tilda settled back to watch the town unfold

before her. 'This is amazing.' Her first trip outside Canada and the USA was turning out to be an adventure already.

Tyres screeched on the tarmac. The tuk-tuk spun around, slammed into a car, then bounced across the road.

Tilda flew out of her seat, saw the road racing up to meet her, just like the brick wall from the past. Her heart pounded and she opened her mouth to cry out, but a strong hand grabbed her wrist, tugging her upward. She jerked her head sideways and skidded along the rough surface on her arm and hip, and banged to a stop against the kerb. Not a brick wall, but it'd hurt all the same. The hand still gripped her wrist.

'What the hell?'

'Tilda? You all right?' The grip loosened but didn't let go entirely.

'Lachlan? That you? What happened?' She pushed up onto her hands and knees.

'Easy. Let's check you out first.' He was right beside her, reaching to take her shoulders in those firm hands.

'I'm good. Might have lost some skin on my arm.' A quick glance. 'Not much.' But her shoulder was beginning to hurt. 'What about you?'

'Took a knock on the hip, but otherwise

think everything's in working order.' He winced as he stood up, rubbing his right hip.

'Seems we got lucky.' Her hands were shaking as she took Lachlan's to pull herself up onto her feet. Her head was light, causing her to sway. 'You caught me.' He'd prevented her face-planting on the road.

'It happened so fast. Hey, I've still got you.' He wound an arm around her waist as she drew deep breaths and her balance returned. 'A car hit the tuk-tuk. Then I think the tuk-tuk banged into another vehicle.'

'What about Kiry? His son?' No, not that cute little boy. He *had* to be unharmed. 'Where are they? Are they all right?'

Lachlan looked over to the vehicle. 'Kiry's inside the upturned tuk-tuk. He looks dazed but okay.' He moved across to him. 'Where's your boy?' he asked urgently, peering around.

'Here,' Tilda called. 'On the road. Under the tuk-tuk.' Dropping to her knees, she leaned close and felt the child's head, then his upper body where the blanket had fallen away. 'Hello?' What was his name? 'Phala?' Was that it? The way she pronounced the name, he probably wouldn't recognise it. Hopefully he'd recognise her tender touch on his cheeks, then his head. 'Lachlan, Phala's unconscious.'

'Kiry's foot is jammed between the pedals

and he's also got a trauma injury at the front of his head.' A crowd had sprung up around them. 'Anyone speak English?' he called.

'Yes.' More than one answer.

'I'm a doctor, this lady's a nurse, but we need urgent help for the little boy. Can someone phone for an ambulance?'

The moment the question was out, people were saying they'd already done that. Lachlan got down beside her, those fingers that had been so gentle on her arm now touching the boy's head, searching for impact injuries. 'There's a soft patch behind Phala's left ear I don't like, and another, smaller one on the back of his head.'

'His breathing's erratic. So's his pulse. Wait…' She touched the boy's cheek. 'Do it again, Phala. He opened one eye for a millisecond,' she told Lachlan in an aside. After waiting a moment she sighed. 'Nothing. Must've been a reflex reaction.'

'Ambulance coming.' A local stood near to them.

'Tell them we have a little boy and his father needing help,' Lachlan said. 'Two stretchers are required—if they've got them,' he added quietly so only she heard.

'Yes, I tell them.' The man pushed through the crowd surrounding them.

'Shall I check the father?' Tilda asked. 'He might be in a bad way too.' He hadn't called out for his boy, and that should've been the first thing this loving dad would've done if he was fully aware of what was going on.

'Do that. We can triage who's worse off, though the paramedics will no doubt do the same. I'll stick with this little guy. He's in a bad way.' Lachlan was lifting an eyelid. 'No one home.'

Her heart filled with worry for the boy, Tilda crossed to the tuk-tuk driver. 'Hello? Can you hear me?'

Kiry talked rapidly in what she presumed was Khmer, leaving her clueless.

'Talk to me in English. I'm a nurse. I was in your tuk-tuk when that car hit,' she reminded him.

More useless words flowed out of his anguished mouth but she only recognised the word Phala.

She shook his arm to get his attention. 'Your son is with a doctor. I need to help you so you can go with him in the ambulance.'

'What's wrong with Phala?' Just like that, he'd flipped languages.

'He landed on the road and has some wounds.' The father frowned. Didn't he know that word? 'He's hurt his head.'

'Alive?'

'Yes.' That was all she was saying. Not that she knew much more, but this man didn't need to be upset any more than he already was. 'Is your leg stuck?'

Tears were pouring down his face. 'Phala hurt? I want to see him.'

'As soon as we get you out of the tuk-tuk.' She looked around, saw two men watching them. 'Can you help, please?' she asked without thinking about languages.

They moved forward.

'This man's leg is caught. We need to pull that steering bar back. Can you do that while I try to move his leg?'

'Yes, we help.'

Between them they managed to move the bar enough for Tilda to pull Kiry's leg free. 'Broken shin bone,' she told Lachlan when he appeared beside her minutes later. 'But I think it's a clean break. I can't feel any splinters under his skin.'

'The paramedics are here and have taken over Phala's care.' He touched the injured leg, and nodded.

'Phala?' demanded the driver as he gasped with pain. 'Where my son?'

'With the ambulance medics.' Lachlan glanced

at the two men she'd got to help and raised an eyebrow.

One nodded, and spoke firmly to the driver.

Tilda then asked him, 'Where do you hurt, other than your leg?'

Again the other guy translated, and then told her, 'In heart. For his son.'

'I'm sure he does.' She blinked back tears as Lachlan began checking over the man's upper body, and saw no reactions to his probing fingers. 'Looks like it might only be his leg that's injured.'

'It'll be enough, considering he needs to be able to drive to make his living. But if it's a clean break it'll only be a few weeks until he's back at work.' Lachlan straightened up as a paramedic joined them. 'This man had his leg caught and Matilda says it's broken. I concur with her diagnosis,' he added crisply. 'She's a nurse.'

'Thank you for helping him and his son.' The paramedic spoke slowly and clearly. 'We take over now. Another ambulance is coming.'

'Of course.' They both stepped out of the way.

'How's your arm?' Lachlan asked.

'Forgotten all about it in the moment,' she muttered.

Again his hand was on her arm, lifting it

to see clearly. 'You've taken a fair bit of skin off. I need some wipes to clean it.' He went over to the paramedic. 'Matilda was also hurt when she was thrown out of the tuk-tuk. Do you have some antiseptic wipes and plasters we could use to clean her up?'

'You were in the tuk-tuk too?' The paramedic looked surprised. 'That's not good. Yes, there are bandages in the ambulance. Come with me, I'll get them.'

'We'll wait until you've got this man on board.'

'No, no. I need a stretcher for him so I'll get what you want at the same time.'

'Want help with the stretcher?'

'These men will do it.'

Within minutes Tilda was walking down the road, once more feeling light-headed now that she wasn't concentrating on helping the driver.

'Welcome to Cambodia,' she murmured.

Lachlan took her arm, drawing her close to that awesome body. 'Been quite the day, hasn't it?'

'Y-yeah.' Her teeth had begun chattering. Probably shock setting in, now that she wasn't focused on helping the little boy. Closing her eyes didn't help. That brick wall from the past returned to her mind. No, it was the road surface. Racing at her, only for her to be jerked sideways. 'Th-thanks again for grabbing me.'

'Sure you're okay?'

'Nothing another hot shower won't fix.' Soaking under warm water to soften her tense muscles had to be a good idea. As long as she could get her clothes off over her head. Her arm was pounding and moving it only aggravated the aches.

'Or a stiff drink,' Lachlan added.

'That also sounds like an ideal remedy.' Might be better than the shower, because then she'd still be with Lachlan.

The hotel receptionist looked up as they entered the front door. 'Hello, Dr McRae, and Miss Simmons. Have you had a nice night?'

I've had better.

Then again, sharing a meal with Lachlan at the club had been pretty darned good. So relaxed and easy.

'It's been great, thank you.'

'That's good. We like guests to enjoy Phnom Penh when they stay here.'

'At least she didn't say guests should have new experiences,' Lachlan chuckled as he kept the elevator door from closing as Tilda stepped inside.

'Your first time being thrown out of a tuk-tuk

then?' she asked. Then laughed and couldn't stop, gulps of laughter bumping up her throat and over her tongue.

'Tilda? Hey, take a deep breath. You're in shock.' He stood before her, holding her upper arms. 'Come on. Breathe in slowly.'

He must think she was hopeless. Might even be wondering how she managed to remain calm in the difficult situations nurses often encountered.

'Sorry,' she gasped. 'I'm fine, really.' She took a deep breath before continuing. 'It's catching up with me. That's all. I keep seeing the road racing towards me before you grabbed me.'

'The same pictures are flashing before my eyes too.' He was staring down at her, his eyes locked with hers.

All laughter vanished. Instead, she was overwhelmed with a sudden need to replace that vision of the road with something warmer, kinder, pain-free. She pressed into his hands still holding her, her head spinning, her breathing slowing. 'I…'

Need to kiss you.

Stretching upward, she began sliding her arms around his neck as though holding onto him would save her from the frightening pictures in her head. She wanted to obliterate the accident from her mind.

Lachlan lowered his mouth to meet hers, touching lightly at first then pressing into her firmly, covering her mouth, sending thrills of anticipation up her spine. His tongue came into her mouth, met hers, caressed. His lips owned hers. She kissed him back with everything she had, and her head spun as she tried to taste more of him. To feel his heat in her mouth. To be one with him. To forget a lot of things from the past. To—

What was she doing? Jerking back, she dropped her arms to her sides. A mortified flush bloomed on her cheeks. 'I'm so sorry!'

The elevator rattled and shook, bumped to a halt. The door squeaked open.

Lachlan loosened his grip on her. 'Tilda? It's all right. It's not every night we get thrown out of a tuk-tuk.'

Tilda. Her head shot up and she stared at him. He'd used her abridged name often. Only those she was close to called her Tilda. Yet she'd told him to use it when they'd only just met. Tilda sounded more special than ever in his deep, sexy voice.

She stepped out of the elevator while digging into her bag for her room key.

He took the key from her shaking fingers. 'I'll clean those abrasions for you.'

A bucket of cold water would've been more useful than that calm voice of his. She'd lost control, he hadn't, and now she needed to get back to how it had been before. They were going to be working together, not having a hot but short fling.

'I can manage, thank you.' She grabbed the key back off him and hurried to her room.

Idiot, idiot, idiot.

CHAPTER THREE

Tilda rolled over and stretched. She touched the other side of the bed. Empty. Good. She had walked away in time before she'd done something even more stupid. Though how she'd resisted the temptation to ask him back to her room when that kiss had been so intense and exciting she wasn't sure.

Lachlan was not the right man for a fling when they'd be working in the same team over here. The accident had brought them together. Work should keep them apart, other than as doctor and nurse. The thing was, she already liked being with him. They were relaxed together and that was enough. Except she'd gone and embarrassed herself last night by throwing her arms around him and kissing him. How would he react to her this morning?

Sitting up too fast, she groaned as aches fired up, letting her know she hadn't come out of yesterday's accident totally unscathed.

Her upper arm was colourful and a little swollen where she'd skidded across the road. She was sore where the skin had been scraped off and there were other aching bruises on her hip and leg, but nothing major. The consequences could've been a lot worse.

Her phone pinged as a text came in.

I'm heading to the airport to pick up Dave. Will let you know when I'm coming by the hotel to collect you. Make the most of the break. We've got surgery this afternoon. Lachlan.

Nothing short about his message. A little smile curved her mouth. He was rather gorgeous, even when she wasn't looking for a man to get all up close and personal with.

She decided she wouldn't even think about last night. At least she hadn't talked too much about herself or exposed her heart and the dreams for her future. But then she never did—other than to James, and look where that had got her. Her dreams for the future were in lockdown, and they were staying there. She so wasn't ready for a rerun of her marriage. Not every man was like him, but how could she tell for sure? She'd stuffed up well and truly once, and once was more than enough for her.

Still, she'd better answer Lachlan. He didn't

deserve to be ignored because of her determination to remain single.

I'll be ready when you get back.

Right now a soak under the shower followed by coffee and breakfast were top of the list to get her day started. Glancing at the dishevelled bed, she laughed with a lightness in her chest that was new. Little more than twelve hours in Cambodia and she'd had dinner at the Correspondents' Club with a man who was rattling her a little too much for her liking, then she'd been involved in a crash and attended to a little boy who'd been seriously injured. If that was how this trip started out, what lay in store for the coming weeks?

In the shower, she soaped her aching body, unable to stop thinking about last night and being with Lachlan, then the accident. How was Phala? And his dad? Was there any way of finding out? She could wait until she got to the charity hospital since he worked there too, but she needed something to distract her from Lachlan.

'Where's the nearest hospital?' Tilda asked the receptionist when she went downstairs in search of coffee.

'The main one's a few streets away. Why—do you need to go there? Are you sick?'

'No. There was an accident with a tuk-tuk last night and a little boy called Phala and his father were hurt. I'd like to know how he's getting on.'

'I know what you say, I heard about it. I will find out where they are and let you know while you have breakfast.'

'Thanks.' It was strange not being able to make a call herself but the chances of finding someone at the hospital to talk to her in English, let alone tell her about their patients, were remote.

The girl came into the hotel café half an hour later. 'The boy is very sick, and the father broke his leg. He's with his son.' She handed Tilda a piece of paper. 'This is the hospital where they are.'

Tilda blinked away the tears threatening to slip down her face. What a kind person this girl was. 'Thank you so much.'

A text arrived. Lachlan.

Twenty minutes away.

Time enough to finish her coffee and eggs, and go upstairs to get her bag. Lachlan seemed as friendly as he'd been before the accident, didn't appear to be keeping his distance since her random attempt to get close and lose herself for a while. If he was willing to forget about it she could relax and enjoy his company, and get on with being a nurse working with him without feeling awkward.

'Stop looking for trouble,' she growled.

Her mouth dried when he sauntered into the hotel lobby a short time later. *Drop-dead gorgeous* came to mind. How well did he live up to that look in bed? It would be fun finding out…

For heaven's sake, Tilda, how are you going to cope for the next two weeks until he leaves?

With difficulty, she suspected.

'Morning.'

She'd manage—by being sensible.

'You look a lot more rested than last night.' His smile seemed tired. Or was that tight? Was her kissing him getting in the way of the easygoing manner they'd established before the accident?

Nothing she could do but get on with the reason why she'd come to Cambodia.

'I'm feeling great. Ready to do some work.' She'd paid for the room, despite being told the charity would take care of it. In her book, money donated to the charity was for the locals in need, not her. The girl on the counter had told her after she'd paid that Lachlan had done the same for his room. Another thing to like about him.

'I'll take that.' Lachlan reached out to lift the pack from her shoulder. 'You must be sore this morning.'

'Not too bad. You?' The aches were still there but nothing she couldn't handle.

'Great.'

As they headed outside she told him about Phala and his father. 'I'd like to visit and see if I can do anything for them.'

'I agree,' Lachlan said. 'Right now we need to get back to the clinic. Dave's plane was late landing and our patient's already waiting for us, no doubt getting more nervous with each passing minute. Be aware that often these people we're helping get very agitated about their operations.'

'Thanks for the heads-up.' It sounded like a different nervousness to what she'd seen with people at home, who were used to regular medical care. For the people the charity was helping, being in the care of foreign doctors and nurses might be a little frightening.

'I haven't forgotten what an eye-opener it was when I first arrived here. Thought I was done with surprises as a doctor. Got that wrong.'

He could admit to being wrong as well? *Go, Lachlan.* James was always right, no matter what.

The front passenger seat was empty. 'Dave's sitting in the back so you can get a good look at where we're going,' Lachlan said as he opened the door for her.

'I've been here before.' The man in the back of the car smiled. 'I'm Dave, by the way. You're Matilda?'

'Thanks, and yes, that's me.' Lachlan's arm brushed against her shoulder as she pressed past, making her feel like cheese melting into a puddle.

The car dipped as Lachlan slid into the driver's seat. The air rapidly evaporated as he shut the door and turned the ignition on.

'We'll drive past the palace on the way out of town. It's worth a visit. I went last week and would like to go back. You want to join me? And anyone else keen to go,' he added almost as an afterthought. Didn't he want to be alone with her? she wondered.

'You bet. If I get the time I've got a list of places to visit, including the palace.' First priority was working at the clinic but she'd been told there'd be occasional days when staff could grab a few hours for themselves. Hav-

ing Lachlan for company would be a bonus.
As long as they remained friendly.

'It's just around this corner,' Lachlan said.
'There—isn't that amazing?'

'Sure is.' The golden roof and spires were
beautiful against the blue sky. The gardens
were neat and pretty, the stairs leading up into
the palace inviting. 'Wow, I've got to see that.
But you don't need to go again. I've got weeks
to do some sightseeing.'

'Sure, but if you change your mind and want
a ride, let me know.'

That'd be a weak moment if she did, she
warned herself. Staying safe and single was her
new mantra. Tilda sat staring out of the window, drinking in all the sights that unfolded
with every turn. People everywhere, vehicles
vying for space on the roads, the Mekong on
its relentless journey south.

'Maybe I should take up travelling permanently. This is fantastic.'

'You wouldn't miss home? Family and
friends to drop in on whenever you wanted
some company?'

There weren't a lot of friends to miss. She'd
run solo most of her life. While in Toronto
she'd been putting her marriage behind her,
not moving on. She hadn't missed James at all.
Seemed her marriage hadn't been what she'd

believed and the freedom in realising that had
given her the strength to live on her own while
staying in touch with everyone who mattered.

'I don't really call anywhere home.'

'You don't have a home of your own? Nowhere in Vancouver?' Lachlan pressed.

'No.' She wished he'd stop asking questions.
They made her uncomfortable.

'Are you returning to Vancouver after this
spell here?' He wasn't giving up.

'Depends on where I land my next job.'

'Hmm.'

She waited for more but Lachlan was suddenly not very forthcoming. She shrugged.

A snore came from the back seat. Dave was
out for the count.

'I've bored him to sleep.' Tilda smiled with
relief. She didn't want everyone knowing she'd
become a bit of a wanderer, and that she had no
reason to settle in one place any more now that
her grandmother had passed, no other family
to stay close to. Her one close friend was taken
up with the love of her life at the moment and
she wasn't going to intrude on them and spoil
things. 'Where's Dave come from?'

'Florida,' Lachlan replied as he concentrated
on the car in front, which appeared determined
to squeeze through a gap only wide enough for
a bike. He winced. 'Only in Asia.'

'You think?'

'I'm guessing. You going to get behind the wheel over here?'

'I doubt it.' She'd far prefer to pay a local or go with Lachlan. He handled driving here with aplomb. Did he handle his plastic surgery cases the same way? Of course he did.

'That's Boeung Kak Lake.' Lachlan pointed beyond the road. 'There're places you can walk along the edge and get some great photos while you're at it.'

'I'll do that next time I'm in this part of town. When I get a day off.' It was taking a while to get very far. 'Walking might be quicker than going by car, though.'

'You're not wrong there. Here we go.' He zipped through a string of stalled cars and swung around a corner onto another road. 'This eventually takes us out of the city centre.'

Shuffling her butt further into the seat, Tilda watched out of the window, enthralled by the different lifestyle unfolding in every direction. People appeared to be constantly on the go, heading in all directions, laden with food bags or children or whatever else they needed.

'The girl I'm operating on this afternoon has third-degree burns to her hands and legs.' Lachlan brought her back to why she was here. 'I am hoping to relieve some of the tightness in her hands today and, if it goes well, next week I'll tend to her legs.'

She couldn't imagine Lachlan not making certain it went perfectly. 'That'll take some recovery time. Will she stay at the charity hospital the whole time?' They wouldn't be able to send her home until the risk of infection was all but gone.

'She's booked in for a minimum of three weeks. Her grandmother will stay with her until she's ready to be discharged. You'll get to show Grandma how to dress the wounds and what to look for in case of infection.'

'Do they speak English?'

He shook his head. 'Not a word, but there's an interpreter at the centre. Anyway, these people are very astute and seem to pick up on anything we need them to understand.'

They were moving along at a steady pace now and the traffic was thinning out, making it easier for him to negotiate his way. He seemed to know exactly where he was going, whereas she knew even if she came the same way once a week over the next month she'd still be none the wiser. Navigation was not her strong point. It was why she had maps galore and a GPS on her phone. Grandma had always teased her by saying she could be spun around in her own bedroom and still wouldn't be able to find the door when she opened her eyes.

Another snore sounded from the back.

She grinned. 'Glad I didn't fall asleep last night when you brought me in from the airport.'

'Think you could compete?'

'I hope not.' She was still tired after her flight and a night that hadn't contained much quality sleep, thanks to recurring images of being thrown out of the tuk-tuk and Lachlan grabbing her in the nick of time.

She glanced sideways again, this time admiring Lachlan's strong chin covered with dark stubble. He looked even better unshaven than he had with his smooth face last night. Sexy as. He was quite the distraction she didn't need. No wonder she'd thrown herself at him.

Squirming with mortification once more, she returned to watching the scenery, feeling a buzz at being in a country so different from Canada. Travelling was starting to look exciting, even when she knew she'd be spending most of her time working. Maybe because of that. Being a nurse was her ultimate career and she never tired of helping people requiring care. There was something so satisfying about seeing a child going from unwell or injured to upright and smiling, or an adult getting back on their feet, ready to face the world again after being knocked down by an accident or illness, and knowing she'd had a hand in that.

A yawn rolled off her tongue. More sleep required—when she had time. Sunlight spilled over her thighs through the windscreen, warm and comfortable. A dog ran across the road, weaving between vehicles, impervious to the danger it was in. She held her breath until it reached the pavement safely, then sighed with relief. Thank goodness for small mercies.

Someone was shaking her gently. 'Wake up. We're here.'

'I didn't snore, did I?'

Lachlan's ensuing grin didn't tell her yes or no.

'Suppose it means I'm boring if both my passengers fell asleep,' Lachlan chuckled as he lifted Matilda's pack from the car. No, she hadn't snored, unlike Dave and the noise he'd made. But to be so relaxed that she'd just drifted off seemed to prove that he didn't affect her the way she'd got to him. He should take heed. He wasn't ready to get close to any woman. Might never be. He hadn't yet let go of Kelly enough for that.

'Welcome to the centre.' Harry held his hand

out to Matilda. 'Glad to have you with us.' Then, 'Good to have you back as well, Dave.'

Matilda shook Harry's hand. 'It's great to be here. I've been looking forward to this ever since I got the acceptance email. Thanks for the info pack. I looked things up online but it's nice to get first-hand knowledge of the area where I'm going to be.'

'You're welcome. I'm sorry about last night's accident. Glad you're all right. Lachlan filled me in this morning. Kiry and Phala are doing as well as expected.'

'Kiry was devastated his boy got hurt.'

'No surprise there, he's a devoted dad,' Harry said. 'Did Lachlan warn you you're up for surgery in a little while?'

Matilda grinned. 'No rest for the wicked, eh? Yes, he did mention it.'

Lachlan's toes curled at the sight of that wide grin. She'd had him wondering if they might become more than colleagues. Careful. A one-night stand was all well and good, but taking it any further than that was not going to happen. He might eventually want another relationship when he'd sorted himself out a bit more, but he doubted it. The fear of losing someone else was still too raw. Anyway, Matilda wouldn't be the right woman. She might be friendly, but she'd clearly been hurt by that horrendous husband of hers, and was probably wary of getting in-volved again, however briefly. 'I'll show you to your room and leave you to unpack before getting down to business in Theatre.'

They all headed in the same direction. The rather basic staff quarters were in a small block next door to the hospital. There were two wards, one for males, the other for females, one theatre and two rooms used for consultations and every other job required with patients. He waved a hand in the direction of a grassed area with outdoor seats. 'Those are some of our pa-tients and their families,' he told Matilda. He was deliberately sticking to calling her Matilda this morning, even inside his own head. Tilda felt too intimate and intimacy between them was not happening, despite the persistent itch under his skin. 'They prefer being outside than in the wards whenever possible.'

Some of the people waved back. 'Hey, Doc.'

Lachlan veered over to them. 'Hello, every-one. This is Matilda, another nurse for you to get to know.'

'Hi, I'm happy to meet you all.'

Everyone chattered at once, then stopped and laughed.

The engaging woman at his side joined in the laughter. 'I'll learn a few words as soon as I can.'

'We say some English,' Kosal told her. 'Not lots.'

'Good. I'll try your language too.'

Lachlan smiled. 'Right, let's get you sorted.' And away from him for a moment or two while he got himself together. Matilda had a way of knocking him sideways when he wasn't even looking for a deeper connection to anyone.

An hour later he was again distracted when Matilda walked into Theatre dressed in blue scrubs, her shiny long hair tied in a ponytail swinging from side to side as she looked around the small but well-equipped room. There was nothing more bland than a nurse's uniform and yet his hormones were doing a frantic dance.

'I'm impressed,' she said. 'I hadn't expected such an up-to-date operating room. We've got all the equipment we need and more.'

'Due to very generous sponsors, I've been told.'

'Talk me through what's happening.'

In other words, cut to the chase. He could manage that. Bringing up the patient's file on screen, he proceeded to outline the procedure he was about to undertake. 'Charlina suffered burns when a pot of boiling oil was accidentally tipped over her. I want to make it possible for her to be able to bend her fingers again.

I'll be taking skin from her buttocks to graft onto the fingers.'

'More scars to fix others.'

'Yep. No other choice, though. It's the downside to this work.'

She touched the back of his hand. 'But you're making things better for her.'

His chest swelled with pride, even when she hadn't said anything more than how it was. 'Thank you.' Right, it was time to get on with doing what he was here for. 'Tilda, this is Sally, our current anaesthetist. She's from Bristol.'

Matilda turned to the other woman in the room. 'Hi, Sally.'

'Hello. Right, are we ready?' Typical Sally, always abrupt and ready to get started. But she was good and he wouldn't want any other anaesthetist—if there had been another—for the operations he did here.

Two and a half hours later he had to say the same for Matilda. She was alert the whole time, never missed a step and had the scalpel or suture thread ready almost before he knew he wanted them.

'Start bringing Charlina round,' Lachlan told Sally. 'I'm finished. Well done, team.' He could look forward to working alongside Matilda over the coming fortnight. She knew her job and did it well. What else could he look forward to with her? He had mentioned going to the palace on a day when they weren't in here with patients. But what about going out for a meal one evening, just the two of them?

Hello? Lachlan? What are you thinking?

She was clearing away the needles and threads, scissors and used swabs. 'Charlina's going to be very sore for a few days.'

He agreed. 'Keep an eye on her pain levels and let me know if she doesn't improve.' Not that he wouldn't be checking on the girl regularly himself, but a second pair of eyes and ears never went astray. 'Her grandmother might talk to you more easily.' He was aware the older women that came to the centre were often wary of talking to foreign males.

Hands on hips, Lachlan stretched up on his toes to ease the tension in his back that came from a long time standing over the operating table.

'You need a massage?' Matilda asked.

Surely she wasn't offering? An image of her hands on his lower back, her fingers rubbing and digging in, turning him on, filled his head.

He hurriedly wiped his mind clear before he embarrassed himself. 'There's a spa just along the road and they're very accommodating of us and the hours we work.'

'I'll check them out. Nothing beats a good

massage.' She was suddenly looking every-where but at him.

'I know what you mean.' Truly. A deep massage fixed a lot of kinks in his body, and after last night's crash there were some new ones to tackle. 'You seem to attract vehicular accidents.'

She blinked. 'Hope I've had my share of them by now.' Looking around, she asked, 'Is that it for today or do we have another patient lined up?'

'That's it, unless Harry has forgotten to mention something, and he's usually on the ball so I think you can safely head out of here and take a well-earned break.' He paused.

Don't ask. Move away.

But his feet were glued to the floor. Words fell out, unimpeded by common sense. 'Want to go for a meal later and try the local food? Wat Danmak is a short walk down the road.'

Her gaze was intense as she looked at him. Over a simple question? Or was she weighing up whether she should spend more time alone with him?

He waited, his heart pounding a little harder than normal. Say yes. Say no. Matilda had got to him when he wasn't expecting her to. But then he had been thinking about her almost non-stop since last night.

'Nearly everyone will come along. It's something of a Sunday night ritual, to download the week with a few laughs over a wine or beer.'

Her smile was tired. 'Then I can't say no, can I?'

Pleased she saw it that way, he suggested, 'Go take a shower and unpack your gear, if you haven't already. One of us will come and get you when it's time to go.'

Her smile was thanks enough. 'Perfect.' With a toss of her head that sent her ponytail swishing across her shoulders, she headed out of the door.

'She fits in well already,' Sally commented.

'Seems to.' Yes, and here he was, wanting her to fit in well with him. When it had looked as if she might turn him down about going out to dinner he'd been reminded to be cautious, yet the moment she'd changed her mind, even if it was to go with the group and not alone with him, his heart had soared.

Showed how much Matilda was getting to him. Too much, too fast. He needed to pull sharply on the handbrake to keep these rampant emotions under control. Just the idea of a fling with her brought him out in a sweat. Sure he wanted one, but it was too risky. What if he couldn't walk away at the end of his time here and forget all about her? He'd have to do that, though. His heart wasn't strong enough to be broken again. What if Matilda's wasn't either? He couldn't do that to her any more than he could make himself vulnerable again.

CHAPTER FOUR

'MORNING, CHARLINA.' TILDA studied the girl curled up against her grandmother and smiled. They looked lovely together. 'How are you feeling?'

The notes showed the last time she was given painkillers was at six that morning. She told the interpreter, 'I'll get her something for her pain in a moment. Can you explain that I am going to change the dressings now?' She was due in Theatre in half an hour but first had to see to Charlina and another patient also post-op. 'Hold your hand out for me. That's it.' This multi-tasking gave a new take on theatre nursing as she got to follow up on how their patients were faring.

Charlina seemed to understand what was required without the interpreter telling her as she held her arm out straight. Apprehension tightened her face and she grabbed her grandmother with her good hand.

'It's all right. I'll be very gentle.' Unwinding the dressing, Tilda exposed the wound. It looked good. No redness or any new swelling to suggest an infection. After cleaning the area around the wound she smoothed on ointment and replaced the dressing with a new one. 'There you go. You're very brave.'

Grandma touched Tilda's arm. *'Saum arkoun.'*

'Thank you,' interpreted the woman standing on the other side of the bed.

'No problem.'

'Charlina seemed uncomfortable when I saw her earlier. How did you find her?' Lachlan asked when Tilda stepped into the pre-op room.

'It's more like a cupboard in here.' She laughed when her arm brushed Lachlan's back as she squeezed past. 'She was very stoic. Her hand hurts a lot so I've given her more analgesics, but when I changed the dressing she didn't flinch once. A little toughie, really.'

Lachlan was reading a file on the computer. 'You get a decent night's sleep?'

'What with the dog fight and those people having an argument outside the building?' It had been very noisy out on the street on and off throughout the night but she had still managed a few hours' rest.

He looked up at her with a wry smile. 'Better get used to it. I don't think there's been one quiet night in the time I've been here. That was a good meal, wasn't it?'

'Good meal, good company.' Just saying. Probably shouldn't have, though, in case he thought she was specifically referring to him, as she'd sat beside him at the restaurant. So much for keeping her distance. Her good intentions didn't work very well around this man.

His eyes widened slightly. 'I agree.'

She really needed to put the brakes on how much she enjoyed his company—and how her body reacted whenever he was around. Unfortunately, she just couldn't stop thinking about how sexy and good-looking he was, and feeling heated and ready for some fun.

'I love the food here.'

'It's not bad,' he agreed. 'Now, our first patient this morning is a thirty-one-year-old man, Dara, with a deformity in his calf muscle after an accident when he was in his teens. The original trauma was put back together too tight and over time it has got worse, making walking difficult and painful.'

'Thirty-one? He's lived with this all that time? That's harsh.' Her heart went out to the man she hadn't yet met.

'That's reality when you're living on the poverty line and have a family to fend for.' Lachlan stood up. 'Somehow he's slipped through the cracks until now. Probably too busy working and looking out for his kids to have time to see a doctor. He's also got a scar on his face I'm going to tidy up.'

Taking a step back from Lachlan, she drew a breath. He *was* too sexy. He tore at her resolve to remain only friends. Another deep breath. If she lifted her hand from her side she'd be touching him. She wanted to. Too damned much.

Turning around, she stepped over to the cupboards and found a set of scrubs to wear. Far more practical and sensible than touching the man who'd tipped her sideways right from the get-go. She could not afford to ignore how James had changed towards her over time. Passion was all very well, but it was the rest of what relationships involved that usually caused the heartbreak.

'Glad he's come to the centre. You'll make things so much easier for him, and he'll be better-looking too.'

'He won't believe what's happened when he tries to walk again,' Lachlan agreed.

'Have you got a physiotherapist lined up?'

'Harry has. She works in the city but does extra work here on the side for nothing. She's a local who trained in Bangkok before returning to her family home.'

'She sounds awesome.'

'No different to everyone here. Including you, with the way you have that relaxes your patients with just a touch or a word, even when they don't understand what you're saying.' He paused, seemed to reflect for a moment, then, 'You're so good at what you do, Tilda. It's early days working together, but I don't see you changing your approach to people.'

Which touched her like nothing had in a long time. Because Lachlan had said it? Perhaps. She couldn't imagine feeling as sensitive about those words if it had been another doctor saying them. But then she'd become so used to James putting her down for most things that for anyone to compliment her was like being given the best present ever.

'Thank you.'

Despite it being a compliment about her work, the excitement tripping along her veins had little to do with work and the doctor, and far more to do with the man delivering it. Did this mean she was opening up to the possibility of another relationship? Of getting close to a man again? Lachlan? Because no other man had made her even start to feel good about herself for a long while. Because she didn't let them. Hadn't been ready. That might be changing, though…

She repeated, 'Thank you.' For what? Being honest and kind? Or for waking her up to a future she'd given up on? Face it. Just because James had turned out to be so controlling didn't mean every man would be the same. Yes, but how did she trust her judgement after getting it so wrong with her husband?

A shiver ran through her, lifted the hairs on her arms. A glance at Lachlan and she was confused. He was a great guy, and this time she wasn't only thinking of his body and how sexy he was. He came across as honest and forthright, genuine and caring. Enough to risk getting closer to? To find out more about him? Not likely. The only way to keep her heart safe was by not putting it out there in the first place. She'd grown up independent, had been strong enough to leave her husband, so why change now?

Because I'd love to have the family I've missed out on so far. Such a short time in this man's company and she was already looking for that? *Give yourself a break, Tilda.*

'Time to get on with the job, Matilda.' He spoke in a steady, serious voice. Probably to bring her back to reality, because he must've guessed that she'd wandered off into a private world of her own. Hopefully he wouldn't realise he had a starring role in her tumultuous thoughts.

Grabbing a clean set of scrubs, she closed the cupboard with a bang. 'I'll be right there.' It was far too soon to be thinking about him like this. Any time would be too soon.

In the bathroom she ignored the persistent worries and ideas her brain was raising and quickly swapped clothes. It was time to go help change Dara's life. Her contribution might not be huge, swabbing and monitoring, but it all added up. So good, Lachlan had said. She hugged herself for a moment. Really? He'd sounded genuine. What was surprising was he had no qualms about saying it.

Sally was talking to Dara, who lay on the operating table when Tilda joined them. The interpreter stood next to her, explaining everything Sally said.

When they paused, Tilda said, 'Hello, Dara. I'm Matilda, your nurse for the operation.'

He blinked, his eyes full of worry.

She touched his arm and smiled. 'I'm going to look after you. I'll be with you when you wake up too.'

'Hello, Dara.' Lachlan had arrived, oozing calmness.

His patient instantly relaxed a little.

Picking up the syringe with a dose of fentanyl, Tilda said quietly, 'Dara, just a little prick in the back of your hand. Start counting to ten.'

The interpreter barely got the words out before Dara said two words, presumably *one, two*, and then nodded off.

'Good to go,' she told Sally.

'Onto it.'

Only the beeping from the monitors made any sound as everyone waited for the anaesthesia to take effect.

Watching the monitors, Tilda saw his heart rate settle, the peaks brought on by the man's fear quietening down. 'Blood pressure normal.'

'He's ready,' Sally said.

Lachlan picked up a scalpel. 'First I'll deal with the facial scar by making an incision to remove the old scar.' He didn't have to say what he was doing, but after yesterday, when he'd operated on Charlina, Tilda understood it was his usual way to discuss the operation with the staff working alongside him.

She liked that, liked knowing what was going on. She hadn't worked with plastic surgeons very often, and it fascinated her what they could do.

'Swab.'

She dabbed the area he indicated. Checked

the monitor. Swabbed some more. Held a small basin out for the scar tissue. Swabbed again.

'I'm doing an incision layered closure. It takes time and is tricky—especially on the face—but gives the best result.'

Didn't she know it? 'He'll be like a new man.'

The theatre went quiet as Lachlan concentrated on repairing Dara's face.

Tilda watched closely as he deftly sutured delicate layer after delicate layer, handing him needles with thread as he required. His fingers never faltered. What would those deft fingers feel like on her skin, winding her insides tighter and tighter with need? The moisture in her mouth dried. She had to get over this obsession with him. One hectic kiss did not change anything.

But it had made a difference to her mindset.

When Lachlan moved onto Dara's leg, time started moving again, and it wasn't long before their patient was wheeled out to the recovery room by another nurse who'd said she'd take over so Tilda could grab a drink before the next operation began.

'What's next?' she asked in general when she returned to Theatre.

'Ten-month-old with a cleft palate,' Lachlan

answered as he scrubbed his hands under the hot tap. 'She's been sent here by a local GP.'

'Poor little tyke. What a way to start life.'

'We've got her early and will soon have her fixed up and looking good. Not to mention able to start to learn to eat normally for her age.'

The moment she saw little Bebe, Tilda fell in love. She was tiny and oh, so cute with big brown eyes watching every move anyone made near her. She didn't cry when picked up and placed on the table, nor when she was injected with a drug to relax her ready for anaesthetic.

'She's beautiful,' Tilda sighed. 'I could cuddle her all day.'

Her hand touched her belly softly. There'd once been a baby in there. Gone in a flash of pain and a load of anguish. It had broken her heart to lose her baby and she'd refused to think about having another. It had hurt too much losing hers to want to risk that pain again. Though that longing for a family had never quite left her, so perhaps one day she might step up and try to get pregnant again. Women had miscarriages and went on to see the next pregnancy through to full term. She couldn't deny she'd love to have a child to love and cherish and watch over as he or she grew up. To have a wonderful man at her side as well would be the best thing ever, but the chances were remote unless she let go of the past and moved on.

'Isn't she just.' Lachlan stood beside her, looking down at the wee girl with longing in his eyes. Did he have similar feelings to hers? What was his background when it came to family?

She hadn't a clue, she realised. Had he been married? Divorced? Children? Still married? No way. He couldn't be. He wouldn't have let her near him at the hotel if he was. Would he? Even when she'd been desperate to get over her shock after the accident in the tuk-tuk and prove she was alive and well, not lying in a hospital or morgue, she didn't think he'd have transgressed if he was in a relationship back home. He didn't seem the type to play around. But what would she know?

'Have you got children?' She had to know. Had to find out a little about him or she'd never sleep again.

'Not really.'

'Huh?' Meaning?

'Wrongly worded. I don't have any of my own. But I do have a lot, and I mean a lot, to do with my friend's three young boys. My best mate died eighteen months ago from a heart attack and I've become their male mentor and role model. Poor little blighters,' he added sadly.

Sorrow swamped her. 'I couldn't think of a better man for the job,' she said huskily.

'You don't know me that well.' His smile was wonky.

'True, but I can't see you as a control freak or you wouldn't be here. Nor can I imagine you're a mean, tough man who expects the boys to jump every time you speak.' Of course she had been wrong before…

'No, they've had enough to deal with without me adding to the pressures they face.' The vinyl gloves snapped as he pulled them on. 'Right, let's get this underway. The sooner we operate, the sooner Bebe is on the road to recovery.'

Personal conversation over. Fair enough. He'd given her enough to think about for now. But she still didn't know if he was single. He'd said *he'd* become part of their lives in a big way, not *we*.

'Fair enough.'

'Are we ready?' Sally appeared at the head of the table.

'Yes.' For once Lachlan didn't talk much.

She could go along with that. She was here to work, not focus on her personal life.

'Bebe,' she said, looking for any response.

'Out for the count, I'd say.' The monitor showed a steady heart rate, normal BP and temperature.

Sally took over, sending the wee girl into a comatose state. 'There you go, Lachlan. All yours.'

He picked up a scalpel. 'Swab her face, please, Matilda.'

They were underway.

'That was a long day,' Lachlan said to the room in general. It was after six and they'd just finished the last scheduled surgery. He was used to long days back in Vancouver, but here the hours seemed more drawn out. Probably because there were fewer medical staff picking up the odd jobs that always came with operations. Nor could he deny the stress from seeing these people's suffering that he didn't often come into contact with at home.

Glancing across the lounge room to Tilda, he saw her covering a yawn. Was it getting to her too? She hadn't held back at all when it came to looking after their patients.

'It seems busier than what I'm used to,' she agreed. 'Yet it's not really. Guess I'm still getting over jet lag.'

Harry opened a bottle of wine and began filling glasses. 'This might help,' he suggested.

'Or send me to sleep at the dinner table.' Tilda laughed.

Her light laugh caught Lachlan's breath. She *was* lovely. When he'd learned who he was picking up from the airport the other day there'd been an inexplicable flutter of anticipation in his gut he didn't understand. A flutter that was getting stronger all the time, despite him constantly reminding himself he didn't want another relationship.

'There you go.' Harry pointed to the glasses. 'Or there's beer in the fridge.'

Tilda took up the offer of wine, as did two other nurses and Sally.

'I'll have a beer,' Lachlan said. 'Anyone else?'

After handing round some drinks, he sank onto the chair furthest from the woman screwing with his mind. She was beautiful, inside and out. Her manner with patients, no matter their age or sex, was what he'd want if he was lying helpless in an operating theatre. Caring and concerned without being OTT. Genuine too. She'd obviously fallen for wee Bebe. A loving look had filled her face as she'd watched over her like a mother hen. There'd been a moment when she'd touched her own abdomen. He wasn't even thinking about why.

His heart squeezed. He and Kelly had discussed having a family once their careers were established. If only they'd known what was coming they might've gone ahead and to hell with their careers. He mightn't have been quite so lost without Kelly if he'd had their child to raise. A mouthful of beer did nothing to soften that thought.

Turning to Harry, he asked, 'You think you'll ever go back home to work in a public hospital?'

'Funny you should ask. I think I'm about ready to give it a go again.' He stared at the floor between his feet for a moment. 'I went through a particularly nasty divorce a couple of years back and took on this position to give myself time to calm down and think about what I wanted for the future.'

Lachlan knew where the guy was at. Different reasons, similar results. 'Sometimes a bit of space works miracles on the mindset,' he said. It was certainly helping his. Even his heart seemed to be shifting, opening up a little—when it really shouldn't.

'Your head needs sorting?' Tilda chipped in, her cheeky grin firmly in place.

'Whose doesn't?' he shot back. But when he looked closer he saw there was a real need to know behind her question. Was that grin her way of hiding her pain from her broken marriage? Or was there something else disturbing her?

'True,' she replied, before sipping her wine. Then she continued, 'I feel as though I've left everything behind in Canada and for now I can get on with doing what I like best without worrying about the future—or the past.'

That was unexpected. Seemed she didn't mind being honest, even if it exposed her inner thoughts.

'I know what you're saying.' That was all he was saying on the topic. He'd said too much already. She didn't need to know about the pressures he faced back in Vancouver.

'After you mentioned there were jobs going, I've just applied for a theatre job at Western General. If I get it, I'll have to start looking for somewhere to live. I'd like to buy a place of my own now that the house James and I owned has been sold.'

He answered without thinking. 'There's always a spare bed at my place if you need somewhere in the meantime. Lots of them, in fact.'

Her eyes widened. 'You want to think about that first?'

See? She read him like a book. He shook his head. 'Not really. I rattle around in a large house and it would be good to have some company. Temporary company, I know, but the offer stands.'

She breathed deep, then smiled. 'Accepted.' Added, 'Thank you. I will get onto looking for a place of my own once I get home. If I get the job, of course.'

'I can't see why you won't.' And that wasn't because there was a shortage of decent nurses. He'd hoped she'd apply to Western G, and had already pre-empted her application and put in a good reference for her via his partners.

A light hue coloured her cheeks. 'Let's wait and see.' Then she looked around the room in general. 'Has anyone here been to Angkor Wat?' she asked.

'I have,' said Harry, sounding grateful for a change of topic. 'It's a bit of a trip to get to Siem Reap but well worth the effort. You can fly, which saves a lot of hassle on the road, but then you'd miss out on seeing so much along the way.'

'It'll come down to whether I have time once I'm finished here. I read that you've got to be careful of the monkeys. They have rabies, so getting bitten isn't wise.'

'That's true, but I don't believe it happens very often. Everyone's warned about the dangers, though there are those who think the monkeys are cute and want to pat them.' Harry laughed. 'Besides, you had a vaccination for rabies before you left home, surely?'

'I did, along with a load of other things.' Tilda turned to Lachlan. 'I'm thinking of going to see Kiry tomorrow when I'm not needed here. I presume he's still in hospital. His boy will be anyway, and where Phala is, I suspect Dad is.'

'Good idea. Mind if I join you?' Lachlan asked. Might as well get to know her better since they might be sharing his house in Vancouver for a little while.

'Of course not.'

'Take the car,' Harry told them. 'Go in the afternoon. The schedule's light tomorrow.'

'Thanks. I can start operating earlier in the morning to make up for it. The patients are already here tucked up in bed.' Lachlan looked at Tilda.

'I'd like that, as long as I'm not causing someone else to have to do extra duties in the ward.'

'Grab the opportunity,' Harry said kindly. 'Someone will want you to cover for them soon enough. That's how it goes around here. All work and no play is not recommended. I work on the belief that if our volunteers get to see something of the country they've come to help in, then later on they'll put their hands up for more chances to do the same.'

'Makes sense,' Lachlan agreed. However, he wouldn't think about 'playing' with Tilda. It was just about checking in on Kiry and his son to see if there was anything he could do for them. Nothing like playing but, come to think of it, any time spent with Tilda was relaxing and enjoyable, and yet at the same time she could wind him up something terrible. That kiss hadn't been relaxing at all. It had been intense and exciting, and probably wasn't going to happen again. She might be happy to spend time with him, as he was with her, but getting too close to one another mightn't be wise. If she did get a position back home at Western General then it would be best for them both to have maintained a purely professional relationship here.

Home. All the problems that he'd needed a break from rushed into his head, reminding him nothing had changed, that they were still there waiting for him. Maybe he should sign up for another twelve months here. Except that wouldn't change a thing. No, in less than two weeks he'd be back in Vancouver, dealing with everyone's persistence about him and Meredith getting together permanently. He knew Meredith was also struggling to stand up to the pressure from her parents. She wasn't a strong woman and desperately wanted someone to take charge of everything for her. Her parents would be ecstatic if they moved in together, as would his. Even when they were kids both sets of parents had wanted them to get married when they grew up. Neither he nor Meredith had ever thought it was a good idea, but with Matt's passing Meredith seemed incapable of fighting them about it.

Tilda was laughing at something Sally had said, a soft, rolling sound that filled him with a sudden longing for love. A love that wasn't conditional on anything, with no demands to do what someone else felt was right. A love that came with genuine care for one another, an understanding that each of them was entitled to be themselves while backing their other half in their life choices. Like he'd had with Kelly. And most likely wouldn't ever experience again. It was too scary to risk his heart again, now he knew how it could all go so horribly wrong.

A tune rang out. Tilda tugged her phone from her pocket and stepped over to the doorway. 'Hi, Janet. How's things? Andy bought you the sideboard? The one you've been hankering after for months? He's in love, for sure.' She was laughing as she talked.

Then Lachlan saw the laughter slip, only to return again a moment later.

'Me? Having a brilliant time. Great people to work with.' Her gaze flicked his way, then away. 'Yes, absolutely. Okay, it's not cheap phoning offshore, I know. Talk again. Bye.' She returned to her seat and picked up her wine, a furrow between her brows.

'All good?' he asked.

Her eyes widened. 'I don't know where Janet—my best friend—finds the time to go to work or fill the pantry, she's so taken with all things Andy. Long may it last.' She turned to answer something Sally asked, sipping her wine with a serious look on that exquisite face.

Lachlan turned away. The longing for more time with her refused to back off one bit. If anything, it had grown. Was Tilda a woman he could have another chance at love with? He felt goosebumps rise on his skin. It was far too soon to be wondering about that, he knew, but hope was a fickle thing. It appeared when he least expected it, and didn't go away when he wished it to.

A clatter of plates being placed on the table dragged him out of his reverie.

'Dinner smells delicious,' Tilda said as she stood up. 'I'm starving.' She looked strong and in charge of her life.

But he'd seen another side to her, seen the despair on her face when her husband had abused her for crashing his car, had seen the hurt at not being cared for, cherished, or even asked how she'd fared in the accident. Was her apparent strength a camouflage for what was going on inside that beautiful head? Was she anywhere near ready to move on to another relationship? Or had she sworn off men for ever? Of course that happened in the early days after a relationship ended, but from what he'd seen with friends in similar situations, it didn't last long. They'd all found new partners and were happy again.

Take note, Lachlan. You too can move on and be happy.

He shuddered. Not likely, with the loss of Kelly forever reminding him how even the strongest love could be shattered. Did that make Meredith's idea a better option? He didn't love her as more than a friend but if anything happened to her it would still be painful for him. No, it wasn't fair to any of them to marry her without love on either side. So he'd return to Vancouver and his career, and the little guys, all on his terms. He wasn't deserting the boys, but neither was he going to be their permanent father figure. Fingers crossed that the man Meredith had mentioned dating a couple of times lately might turn out to be right for her and the boys.

'Coming?' Tilda called from the other side of the room, a laden plate in her hand.

He laughed, putting aside everything but the here and now. 'You really are starving, aren't you?' This relaxed feeling came so easily when he was around her. It made him happy. He'd enjoy it over the coming days, and to hell with anything else.

As he placed a full plate on the table next to her, his phone pinged. Sitting down, he swiped the screen and saw a photo of the boys. They were laughing, and no doubt shouting, with their arms in the air as they leapt off the deck. His heart melted at the sight of the guys. He did love them. Matt's lads were very special.

'You okay?' Tilda asked softly.

He held the phone so she could see the picture. 'My mate's kids.'

'Aren't they gorgeous? Wow.' She looked away. 'It must be so hard for them to lose their dad.'

'Sure is.' Another ping and another photo arrived. Meredith dressed to the nines in tight jeans and an off-the-shoulder blouse, a wide, determined smile on her overly made-up face. No, he wasn't being nasty about her, he was just over it all. 'His widow,' he told

Tilda tiredly. Though why he'd shown her the photo was a bit of a mystery. He didn't want her thinking Meredith meant more to him other than as Matt's widow.

'She's lovely,' Tilda said, sounding thoughtful. Trying to figure out where he fitted into the picture?

'Matt fell for her in a blink.'

'I can see why.' She forked up a mouthful of rice and vegetables.

'She's been struggling to move forward since he died, and likes me there for her a little too much.' There, he'd put it out there. Some of it anyway.

Tilda took his phone out of his hand, and flicked the screen back to the photo of the boys. 'These are the ones who get to you, who've touched your heart. It was there in your face the moment you saw the photo. They're important to you. I might be wrong, because I know nothing about you and what's been going on, but I think they're lucky having you on their side. Nothing else is as important.'

Was it all right for a man to cry? In front of his colleagues? All over a few words this woman had said. Because she'd somehow got to the heart of his woes without digging for information. She seemed to understand him instinctively.

'Thank you.'

She shrugged eloquently. 'It's true.'

Shoving up to his feet so fast his chair crashed to the floor behind him, he swore. 'Damn it.' Tilda read him way too easily and he didn't like it. Returning the chair to upright, he headed for the door and air that wasn't tinged with Tilda's scent. Sweet with a little bit of sharpness. Tilda to a T.

Outside, the air was hot and stifling, vehicle and other smells real and unattractive. Just what he needed to get back on track. Matilda Simmons could not become a part of his future. He wasn't ready to let her anywhere near his heart.

Even if it felt like she'd already started knocking on it.

CHAPTER FIVE

'HELLO, KIRY,' LACHLAN said to the man stretched out on the hospital bed with Phala swathed in a small blanket tucked against his chest. 'How are you?'

Tilda watched Kiry's eyes widen and a lopsided smile begin to spread across his mouth. 'How's Phala?' she asked. It had been a busy week since the accident and today was the first time they'd been able to get back into town.

The smile faded. 'He's still sick. I'm sorry for crash. Are you hurt?'

'Don't say sorry. It wasn't your fault that other car hit the tuk-tuk.' At least she didn't think so, but then she had to admit she hadn't seen the car coming and was only going on what bystanders had told them at the time. 'We didn't get hurt,' she added.

'That's good. I worry.'

'Don't worry any more.' Lachlan stepped closer. 'How's your leg?'

'My leg break but already mending well. Phala much worse. His head hit and he sleeps a lot.' He twisted his head to look over to a small woman curled up on a mattress on the other side of the bed. 'My wife, Bopha.'

The woman blinked sleepy eyes. 'Hello.'

Kiry rattled off something in his language and the woman pulled herself upright.

'Hello.' Tilda held her hand out. 'I'm Matilda, and this is Lachlan.'

Bopha's hand was small in hers as Tilda squeezed it gently. 'Sorry if we woke you, but we wanted to see how your husband and baby are.'

Again Kiry talked to his wife, and she reached up to hug Tilda.

'My wife work here at night.'

And was sleeping beside her family by day. It must be exhausting, Tilda conceded. Not to mention what worrying about her little boy did to her. Lachlan had already talked to a doctor and learned Phala had suffered concussion and a small skull fracture. The good news was that he should recover relatively quickly with no serious side-effects.

She returned Bopha's hug. 'Can I do anything for you?' she asked instinctively.

Bopha looked to her husband, who spoke to her.

He interpreted her reply. 'You have been kind coming to see us. Thank you.'

'How long before you can work?' Lachlan asked him.

Tears welled up in Kiry's eyes. 'Few weeks to fix leg. Tuk-tuk broken.'

'Where is it? At a garage?'

A frown appeared on Kiry's forehead. 'Garage?'

'To fix tuk-tuk.'

'Ahh. Yes, at garage. But no fix. No money.'

Tilda's heart plummeted. These two worked so hard to make ends meet and now they'd lost one important source of income. 'Can—'

Lachlan caught her hand, squeezed lightly. 'Mind if I talk to him about this? Man to man,' he added quietly.

She got it. Male pride was important here. Whatever Lachlan was about to say, it would be better coming from him. 'Go for it.' She moved nearer to Bopha, who was hugging Phala close 'He's lovely,' she said. Just as cute as the first time she'd seen him, despite the crepe bandage wound all over his head.

His big brown eyes followed her every move, his little mouth curved into a smile that sent ripples of longing through her. Why, here in Cambodia, were little children tripping her heart and making her wish for another chance to have a baby? It wasn't as if she was in a position to have a child. No permanent job, even if that would be easy to fix. No home—again, a little effort would sort that. She had some savings and although she couldn't afford to buy the place of her dreams, she could buy a small apartment for the two of them. No family to support her and love her baby. Her heart sagged. No easy answer to that one.

'Tell me where the tuk-tuk is. I'll go and see if they can fix it now,' Lachlan was saying. 'I will get it done for you.'

'No, not for you to do. I had accident, you and lady hurt.'

'We are all right,' Lachlan reiterated. 'No broken bones, no cuts or sore places.'

Phala chuckled when Tilda tickled his chin, careful to be gentle. When his mother held him out to her, she happily held him against her, his small, soft body tucked against her as though she was used to holding little ones so close. If only. This sudden drive to have a baby was a little overwhelming. Realistically, she wasn't sure she was even in a position to become a mother. She'd have to keep working should she choose to have a baby and she'd want to be at home with it all the time, but then other women managed to be single parents, so why not her? Choose being the operative word here.

Becoming a parent needed to be thought about in depth to make sure she was in a position to give her child the life he or she deserved.

Lachlan's steady voice cut through to her. 'I'll see what needs to be done to the tuk-tuk. I... We—' he inclined his head towards Matilda '—we would like to help your family.'

Relieved to be distracted from her rather unsettling thoughts, she concentrated on what he'd just said. They hadn't discussed this but he'd picked up on her need to do something for these people. She gave him a nod, although whether he noticed she wasn't sure, as he was focused on Kiry. Was this why she was suddenly thinking about babies? Because Lachlan was touching her so deeply? It was a huge leap to go from feeling a little closer to him, to then having a baby on her own. A gigantic leap. One with no certain landing.

'So would other people at the hospital where you work,' Lachlan continued.

'No. We manage,' Kiry told Lachlan stubbornly. Kiry didn't know he was up against a determined man who she suspected was used to getting his way. How long before the father gave in? Her eyes on Phala and her ears listening to Lachlan and Kiry dispute the matter, she smiled and waited. Bopha seemed to be waiting too, though how she understood what was going on was anyone's guess.

'I know, but let us help.' Lachlan waited with the air of a man who would stay there all day, if need be.

The silence stretched out.

'I get nurse to write address for you,' Kiry finally said with a sigh.

'Thank you.' Lachlan glanced across to her and the child in her arms, and a smile split his face. 'He's beautiful.'

He might've said *he*, but she got the feeling he was including her in that comment. Or was that too much to expect? Whatever, she'd accept how his words made her feel warm and happy, and leave it at that.

'Phala's gorgeous,' she agreed.

'Do you mind if we go and see the mechanic who's supposed to fix the tuk-tuk while we're nearby?' Lachlan asked Tilda as they headed back to the car from the hospital, already guessing she'd say yes. She was just as invested in looking out for the driver and his family as he was.

'Of course not. Getting the tuk-tuk back on the road is important.'

'Exactly.'

'Want me to put the address of the garage in the GPS?' Tilda asked once she was in the car.

'Here you go.' He handed her the piece of paper the nurse had written the details on. 'Hope it's easy to reach. I don't fancy ducking and diving in this traffic for too long.' It seemed more chaotic than usual.

A pert eye-roll came his way. 'Pull up your big boy pants, will you?' She tapped the address into the GPS and ping, there it was.

As simple as that. 'How did anyone get around cities before GPS was invented?'

'By dogged determination and pulling their hair out.'

'That'd work well here when we don't know a word of Khmer.' Starting the car, he indicated to pull out and then went for it. It was the only way to get around here, he'd decided on his first time behind the wheel. Hairy, but it got the right results. Seemed the locals had six eyes in their heads because they usually managed to avoid banging into other vehicles. Hopefully they'd keep an eye out for him so he'd be safe. And Tilda. He didn't want her getting hurt again. She'd had enough knocks in the past year.

'In one hundred metres turn left.'

'Yes, ma'am.'

'In fifty metres turn left.'

'Onto it.'

'Turn now. Then in two hundred metres turn right.' The clear American voice continued directing him and within fifteen minutes they were pulling up outside a shed with tuk-tuks and cars parked in all directions.

'This looks like it.' Lachlan sighed with relief. 'Now to find out what's being done about Kiry's tuk-tuk, if anything. I presume you're coming in with me?'

'What if there's no one who speaks English?' was her answer as she opened the door.

'Then we're in trouble.'

'Hello, can I help you?' a man called out in English from the shed as they approached.

'Problem number one sorted,' he said to Tilda. 'Yes, we're looking for the mechanic who's got a tuk-tuk that was in an accident several nights ago. Kiry owns it.'

'I have it here. What do you want to know?' A tall, slight man sauntered across. 'It's badly damaged. It will cost a lot to fix.'

Holding his hand out to him, Lachlan explained. 'We were in it when it crashed. Can we have a look at it?'

'Of course. Come around the back.' The man led the way past other vehicles to the one they'd come to look at. Inside the large shed there were five mechanics at work on various vehicles.

'You're busy,' Lachlan noted.

'Always accidents on the road,' replied the man mournfully.

So much for thinking driving was reasonably safe if he just paid attention! 'I am constantly on edge when driving here.'

Beside him, Tilda gave a laughing huff. 'Now he says it.'

'Here it is.' The man pointed. 'See how the front is completely crushed in? That can be straightened but the strength will be compromised.' The metal frame had bent and twisted, underlining what the man said.

'So another hit at the front would have even worse consequences?' He hated to think how that little boy would fare then. The wrecked tuk-tuk gave him the heebie-jeebies just looking at it. An idea was already slipping through his mind.

'I can replace the whole framework but it will be expensive for Kiry. I am going to see him tomorrow and ask what he wants done.'

'He needs it to be repaired so he can get back to work once his leg is healed, or how else is he going to earn a living?' Tilda's voice sounded full of tears.

A quick glance her way showed he wasn't far wrong. She was a softie through and through.

Turning to the mechanic, he asked, 'How much to fix it properly?'

The sum he was given didn't help, because he had no idea if it was a good quote or not. Doing a quick calculation in his head, he then asked, 'How much is a new tuk-tuk?' There was a yard full of shiny new ones next door.

The man smiled and told him.

Again Lachlan had no idea if that was good or crazy high. 'Thank you. I'll do some research and get back to you.'

'Would you like to use my office?' The guy wasn't giving up easily. He had a living to make too and, despite the busy garage, he'd want every sale he could make.

Tilda had her phone out and already had information popping up on the screen. 'Nothing in English that I can find.'

'I'll ring Harry, get him to look up what I want to know. He can get the interpreter to tell me prices.'

It took a while but finally he had the answers he needed. 'I need to check that Kiry's okay with this before finalising the deal. I'll phone you tomorrow,' he told the garage owner.

They shook hands, and he headed back to the car with Tilda.

Lachlan held the door open for her, happy to be able to solve Kiry's problem for him. It might take a bit of convincing to get him to accept that this was the better way forward, but he'd leave that to Harry to sort out since he knew the man way better.

'Feel like stopping in at the club for a drink?'

'Yes, I do.'

As simple as asking. No hesitation for once. 'Good.'

So much for holding Lachlan at arm's length. Tilda sighed as they entered the club. She'd said yes without thinking and, to be honest, she was happy spending time away from the hospital with him. It had been a busy week, with the list of patients never seeming to get any shorter. She could go for a meal with any of the staff but it was Lachlan she most wanted to be with. For now she'd run with that and give up questioning her every thought.

'I'll have a water. What would you like?'

'Beer.'

Leaning forward, she gave the barman their order and sat back. 'What you've done for Kiry and his family is special.'

Those firm shoulders shrugged. 'No big deal.'

It was, but she knew when to shut up. Or what to be quiet about anyway.

'I can't imagine how hard it must be for them at the moment without half their income.'

'Very difficult, I'd say.' He picked up the glasses the barman placed in front of them. 'Let's sit by the windows and watch the city going by.'

Okay, so he didn't want to talk about Kiry.

'Good idea.' She followed him to a table overlooking the street below with the river beyond. 'Are you looking forward to getting back home? Seeing those gorgeous boys?'

He took a large mouthful of beer and set the glass down carefully.

A topic she shouldn't have raised? 'Tell me to shut up if I've touched on a sensitive subject.'

'Tempting as that is, I'll restrain myself.' His smile was tight, but it was still a smile, and directed at her what was more. 'I'm getting so much out of being here and the work I'm doing. It's been an eye-opener. In that respect going home will feel a bit like deserting the cause.'

Funny, but she had a feeling it was going to be much the same for her when the time came to board the plane headed back east.

Lachlan gazed outside as he continued. 'I came here because I needed to do something for myself. The past year and a half have exhausted me.' His chest rose on a breath. 'No, that's not true. I was shattered before that. My wife died two and a half years before Matt.'

Whoa. How much could a man take and not break apart completely?

'I don't know what to say, Lachlan.' She placed a hand on his arm. 'It's beyond comprehension.' His skin was warm, while hers was heating up. At such an inappropriate moment too. She gently removed her tingling hand.

'It was. Often still is.'

'I bet.' She sat quietly, leaving it up to him to continue talking or to leave it alone.

'I decided to take a little time out to come here so I might figure out what I want for myself in the future. I haven't come up with all the answers yet, but it's been good getting away from everyone for a break.'

'You look happy and keen to be doing things, like you've recharged your batteries.'

'I do feel marvellous. I get up in the morning smiling. It's been a while since I did that.'

'So what's the problem?'

His mouth flattened. 'Meredith emails and texts regularly, keeping me up-to-date with every little detail about the boys.'

'Why?'

'She wants more than I'm prepared to give. I

thought me coming away would give her time
to think it through. Focus on dating this other
guy she's been telling me about.'

'What does she want from you?'

He drained his glass. Plonked it on the able,
looked around, nodded at the barman before
looking back at her.

'She'd like us to get married. It would make
everything easier for her.'

Her heart thumped. No way. Talk about putting unfair pressure on him. But then what did
any of it have to do with her? She and Lachlan had nothing going on between them. The
fact she couldn't stop thinking about him night
and day did not constitute a relationship. Just
a messed-up head on her part.

'You're not keen on the idea?'

'Not at all. She's not my type and, if she's
being honest with herself, I'm not hers either.'

*What is your type? Down, girl. Wrong place
and time for that question, if there'll ever be
a right one.*

'Why's she so adamant on marrying you,
then?'

'She's a bit lost. Trying to pick up the pieces
and keep moving forward is hard. We grew
up with each other, saw one another all the
time. Our parents are best friends,' he added.
'They'd all love it if we got together, and are

adding to the pressure, which only makes it more difficult to get Meredith to back down.'

She grimaced in sympathy.

'That still doesn't make it right though. I'm just not interested in her that way.' He sighed. 'I've probably added to the problem by keeping a lot of things going in that household. Too much. But Matt was my best mate. He'd have done the same for my family.'

Tilda found herself sighing with sadness for Lachlan. To have to deal with this must be like walking a tightrope. 'What a position to be in.' Her hand was lying on top of his without her realising she'd reached out to him. 'Stay true to yourself, Lachlan. Otherwise it's a recipe for disaster.'

'I know. Still doesn't make it any easier. It doesn't help that our parents are backing her.'

'Stay true to yourself,' she reiterated.

'I intend to.' Did he realise he'd turned his hand over and was now holding hers? Was he being true to himself?

Or was that simply wishful thinking on her part? Whichever, it felt far too good. So she removed her hand and picked up her glass. 'Cheers to better things ahead for us both.' Her future career was at least looking up. 'I heard first thing this morning that I got that position at Western General. That was quicker than I'd expected.'

'I knew you would. Well done. Guess that means I've got a roommate for a few weeks at least.'

'You bet. I have looked at places to buy on-line but it's going to be easier to sort that out once I get back to Vancouver.'

'Take your time. The spare rooms aren't going anywhere. Are you looking forward to returning home?'

'Yes. It's time.'

'I'm glad for you.' He drained his beer and nodded to the barman for another one.

'Looks like I'm driving back to the centre tonight. Should be interesting.' She dug deep for laughter, needing to lighten the atmosphere. Now he'd told her about Meredith she felt defensive for him, and for herself. She liked Lachlan a lot. Possibly too much after such a short time, but it was how it was. Funny how she wanted to support him when she didn't really know him that well. It was an instinctive feeling, same as the one that told her she should trust him. That he would never be like James, demanding everything be about him.

'Hope you're good at looking out for all those vehicles that'll be coming at me,' she said when they got back in the car.

'It's a bit like walking through the traffic as you cross the road—stick to your plan, don't suddenly veer off in either direction and you'll be fine.'

It wasn't anywhere near as simple as that. Tilda held her breath as she manoeuvred between a tuk-tuk and another car, and still couldn't relax her lungs as a woman walked out in front of the car. Eyes right, left, right, steer left, straighten, steer left again, straighten.

'You've got this.' Lachlan was back to being relaxed. 'You're a natural.'

'You think? I'm shaking.'

'We're still in one piece, and once you turn the next corner the traffic will thin out.'

'What corner? Which side?' Her head spun one way, then the other. 'Tell me.'

'Easy.' His hand touched her thigh, making her jerk sideways. 'Move towards the right. You've got about two hundred metres to the corner.' His steadying hand gave her confidence.

She could do this. 'There? Where that truck is turning?'

'That's it.' Lachlan was alternating between watching her and checking out the traffic ahead. There was laughter in his voice as he removed his hand.

Come back, she thought.

'You should be terrified,' she muttered.

She was. Though not quite so much now she was getting the hang of all this uncontrolled traffic. When in Phnom Penh, she thought and laughed aloud, pressing the accelerator harder. Then they were around the corner and she could see gaps in the traffic and wasn't being cut off from all directions. Her breathing eased and the thumping in her chest began quietening.

'I'm beginning to enjoy this.'

'Look out for that dog,' Lachlan said sharply.

They both jerked forward when she braked.

'Hell, and here I was thinking this was fun. Maybe not.' The dog was running between two cars and horns were blaring and arms waving. 'Don't tell me if it gets hit.'

Silence.

Oh, no. Please don't let it have been hit.

'He's made it. Now he's racing along the footpath.' Lachlan grinned and returned to watching the road. 'Next turning on the right.'

It might've become fun driving through the mayhem that was Phnom Penh's roads, but when she parked outside the clinic she heaved a massive sigh of relief. 'Phew. We made it back in one piece. Think I'll stick to letting other people drive me around from now on.

I've probably grown a few grey hairs in the time it took to get here.'

Lachlan leaned over and looked at her head. 'Can't see any. Still looks dark brown and shiny to me.'

Her eyes met his, and again her breathing stalled. There was a heady mixture of caring and heat in his gaze. The need to kiss him, to be kissed in return, swamped her. 'Lachlan—'

'Shh.' He took her face in his gentle hands, his thumbs making small circles on her cheeks. Leaning closer, he placed his mouth over hers. His kiss was soft and warm, and then it wasn't. It became hard and hot, stealing the air out of her lungs and setting her heart alight with desire. Waking her up fast, underlining why she'd been attracted to him right from the start.

She sank into him, returning his kiss with all she had. It was so easy to give him everything. It was what it was, and she couldn't be more relaxed—and tense—as her lips felt his, her tongue warred with his. And her body heated up and tightened everywhere.

Then he was pulling back, locking an intense gaze on her. 'We'd better stop while it's possible.'

She didn't think it was. 'But—'

'But we're outside the clinic's sleeping quarters, and there's no way we can follow through without everyone knowing. That might not be the best idea we've had.' Longing was blazing in his eyes and going straight to the centre of her desire. 'Plus anyone walking by can see us and that might not go down too well with the locals. We are meant to be a little circumspect around here.'

Flopping back into her seat, she nodded. 'You're right.' But did he know how to get her going, or what? One touch of those lips on her mouth and she'd melted—needing him, wanting him, having to have him. Only she wasn't going to be able to do that.

Damn, damn, damn. They also couldn't do this when they were going to share his house for a while. Platonic was the only way to go.

'Tilda—' Lachlan's hand covered hers '—I'm really sorry. I want to follow through with more kisses and whatever else you're comfortable with, but at the same time you're coming to stay with me and we're going to be working in the same hospital, and that could get a little too intense for both of us.' He continued looking at her, and she could see his mind working overtime behind those intense blue eyes. 'It's probably for the best.' He sounded as though he was trying to convince himself more than her.

'I have no intention of getting deeply involved with you or any other man.' Though she knew very well that she'd already begun to wonder if she'd got that wrong.

'But...' The word hovered between them, filled with temptation.

He was still watching her. The tip of his tongue appeared between his lips, and then, as though he couldn't bear not to, he leaned back in and his mouth covered hers once more.

She froze. Damn, but she wanted to kiss him back. But she also wanted to protect herself and walk away. Kiss him. Walk away. Kiss him.

He jerked his head back. 'What am I thinking? I've got to stop this. I've got enough problems as it is.' He elbowed the door open.

'So I'm a problem now?' she snapped.

He turned to look at her. 'Tilda—Matilda, unfortunately, yes, you are.' Then he got out, closed the door quietly and walked away.

What sort of problem? A good one? A bad one? Hell, he'd been talking about his problems at home and that had sounded bad. Now she was a problem, so that had to be bad too. Great. Tilda shoved the door open and leapt out. Her head was pounding with frustration and disappointment.

One minute they'd been kissing like there was no tomorrow. Turned out there would be no follow-up. Lachlan had called it quits on their kiss. The fact he'd probably done the right thing didn't make her feel any better. She'd wanted him. Longed to go to bed with him. To have hot, mind-blowing sex with Lachlan. She mightn't want a man in her life permanently, but she could spend the night with one for a few hours, enjoy some relaxation and fun. With this man in particular.

But it wasn't going to happen. That hurt. Being turned down stung. When it had no right to. Tomorrow she might be grateful for his action, but tonight she was peeved and hurt and frustrated. Tomorrow she'd agree with him, but not tonight. If they had followed through on that kiss it would only add an unbearable tension to their relationship. From what he'd told her about his home life, more tension was the last thing he needed. She could accept that, and support him as necessary. She could also feel sad and disappointed they hadn't succumbed to temptation. She was only being human.

'Damn you, Lachlan McRae. Damn you to Vancouver and back. You're not walking away from me. Not tonight.' Tilda ran after him. 'Lachlan. Wait.'

He slowed but didn't stop.

She caught up and grabbed his hand, kept walking at his pace. 'You're right. Neither of us wants a relationship. But we both want each other.' She could've gone on but was suddenly overcome with a rare shyness.

Lachlan remained silent.

'I'm not trying to force myself on you.' She hadn't got through to him; instead it sounded as if she was begging. She stopped and pulled her hand away. Tried to, but suddenly she was being swung into his arms and held tight against that solid body.

'You're right, damn it. I do want this.' His hot lips claimed hers, devouring her, making her knees weak.

Corny, but too true to ignore. Her head spun with the hot sensations swamping her. Pressing into him, she kissed him back like there was no tomorrow. Gave him everything she had with her lips and tongue.

Then he was pulling away again, his arms still holding her but not so close. His chest was rising and falling faster than normal. 'Damn it, Tilda. Where did you come from?'

'From a broken heart,' she whispered.

'Me too.' His hands fell away. 'We're rushing into this, Tilda. It might only be kisses, but when I kiss you I feel like I'm opening myself up to being vulnerable, and I'm not sure I'm ready to do that just yet. I don't want you to be hurt either.'

She got the message loud and clear. They were not following through on those blinding kisses. Not tonight. But she wasn't letting him go either. Not yet.

'I understand. It is a little scary.'

'You think?' His laugh sounded more like a bark as he took her hand and led her back to the hospital, and relative safety from her need to throw caution to the wind and leap on him, pull him to the ground and have her wicked way with that stunning body.

Lachlan was right about one thing. They could both get hurt. Neither of them needed or deserved that. But he was still holding her hand. Did that mean he wanted to follow up on those kisses and get closer to her, despite his misgivings? Only time would answer that.

She had to know more about him before giving into the longing filling her. A longing she was coming to suspect would take a lot to fulfil. A fling mightn't do it. If they even got that far. There was a lot more to Lachlan she had yet to learn, and that was needed to keep her heart safe from another mistake like James had been. She'd be an absolute fool to think another man wouldn't hurt her. She wanted love and a family so much that she was at risk of ignoring the clues and leaping right on in.

There'd only be herself to blame if she got it wrong again.

'Time will tell.'

'It's been great working with you, Lachlan. I hope you put your hand up to volunteer with our charity again.' Harry raised his glass and everyone followed suit.

'To Lachlan.'

Tilda swallowed a large mouthful of wine and set her glass down.

To Lachlan.

She was missing him already. 'Time will tell,' she'd declared. But it hadn't changed a thing so far. The past week since those heart-stopping kisses had whizzed past in a blur of work and more work, with a few more kisses thrown in. Holding back the passion bubbling inside her had been the most difficult thing she'd done in a while. She had to constantly remind herself she wasn't ready to let go of the deep mistrust of men she still carried.

Lachlan hadn't been forthcoming in giving more of himself either, and seemed to easily rein himself in whenever their kisses got too intense. Now he was heading home.

He was talking to Harry. 'I most certainly will volunteer again. It's been a great adventure and I've got so much from it.'

Pick me.

Tilda shivered. He was everything she wanted in a man—if she could let go of the fear of making another mistake.

'No more than you've given.' Harry grinned.

Lachlan flicked her a quick hot look. Reciprocal heat flared in her cheeks. She reached for her glass to down something cool. So much for staying in control of her emotions. But then she hadn't been very good at that whenever Lachlan was around. Who'd have thought only a fortnight ago she'd be so easily flustered by him? She'd be lonely once he'd gone.

Sally was unpacking platters of takeout food.

'Want a hand?' She reached for a brown paper carry bag.

'Cheers.'

Time was flying past. Before she knew it the taxi would be here to take Lachlan to the airport and the next time she saw him he'd be her temporary landlord. Should've had a fling while they could. A short-term arrangement that would've finished tonight and at least she'd have satisfied the restlessness in her heart.

As the meal came to an end Lachlan came across to her. 'Come and join me outside for a few minutes before my taxi arrives?'

Breathing in that sexy male scent that was him, she nodded. 'Going to give me the rules for living in your house?' she teased.

He took her hand. 'I really wanted to have a few minutes alone with you without everyone else around.'

'Are you ready to go home?'

'Sort of.' His chest rose slowly on a long intake of air. Then he let it go and gave her a blinding smile that sent heat rushing to her toes and everywhere else. 'I should warn you that the boys and Meredith drop in and out of my place a lot. As though it's their own house, really.'

'That's fine, I understand. Is Meredith still pestering you to marry her?'

'A little.'

This Meredith thing had to stop. It wasn't fair to Lachlan.

'How will she react to me being in your house?'

'Probably won't make any difference to her end goal.'

An idea was forming in her head. Dare she put it out there? Chances were Lachlan would think she was crazy and immediately withdraw the offer of a room, but she badly wanted to help him. He deserved to be left in peace, if that was what he wanted.

The words fell from her mouth in a rush. 'Won't me staying there really make any difference at all?'

'I doubt it. I've been completely blunt in the past and it still hasn't changed a thing.'

'What if we pretended to be getting married? Say that's why I'm moving in?'

Lachlan stared at her, shock widening his eyes for a long moment. Then he gave her a small, heart-tugging smile. 'You're serious?'

'You're helping me out with an offer of somewhere to stay. I want to do something for you.'

'But pretending to be my fiancée? You'd really go that far?'

'It's more about how far *you're* prepared to go. It's your family and friends we'd be facing up to. Of course it doesn't totally fix the problem, because it would only be a fake engagement, but it might give everyone time to stop and think about what they're wanting of you. Or give Meredith the incentive to focus on the guy you told me about that she's supposed to be dating.'

The next thing she knew, she was being swung up in his arms as he spun her around the deck. Then he placed her on her feet and leaned in for a kiss. 'Oh, Tilda, you are full of surprises.'

'That's a yes then?'

'A very big yes. But if I—or you—change our mind before you get home then that's fine too.'

Her heart was thundering in her chest. What had she done? Funny how she didn't really care. She was stepping out of her comfort zone for Lachlan and it felt good. There might be no stopping the kisses and where they could lead once she reached his house, but that might be for the best. She could find out how she really felt about him. She shrugged off the insidious thought that she already knew and was making herself dangerously vulnerable.

'Tilda?'

'Yes?' Then she spoilt the seriousness by grinning. 'One day at a time, eh?'

He held his hand out, ran a finger over her lips. 'Done deal, Tilda.' There were sparks in his eyes as though he was trying not to smile too much.

Tilda. Her nickname sounded so sexy coming off his lips. A softening started expanding inside her heart, raising hope for more between them than just a room in his house. Because if they were pretending to be engaged then they'd most likely need to share a bedroom, wouldn't they? So maybe they should just go ahead and have a real fling? Get this desire out of their systems and move on.

'You're wonderful, you know?'

'Absolutely.' She laughed, feeling on top of the world. Then she suddenly sobered. 'Are we doing the right thing? It does seem a little OTT. I'd hate for anyone to get hurt by our actions.'

'You're helping me out of a difficult situation that just won't go away. I hope when we come clean and admit what we did, everyone will finally accept how serious I am about not wanting to settle down with Meredith. Honestly, I don't believe she really wants it either. It's just the easy option for her.'

Reaching up, she kissed him. 'Then we'll see it through and, who knows, maybe we might have some fun along the way.'

More kisses, because fiancées kissed their guys, didn't they? Even fake ones? She'd make sure they did.

CHAPTER SIX

Hi. How's it going over there? Been to see any other tourist sites? I miss the city and all the noise and smells. It's strange being back at work here after the charity hospital. More papers to sign off, for one. Looking forward to you getting here. Lachlan.

HE WAS? GREAT, Tilda thought, because she missed Lachlan far more than she would've believed.

Hitting reply, her fingers began answering his email.

Sally and I went out to the Killing Fields yesterday. Very confronting. We've got a lot of general surgery patients this week as that's the specialty of the surgeon who replaced you. Charlina was discharged successfully, so that's good. And Phala and his family are now back at home too.

My start date at Western G is the Wednesday after I get to Vancouver. I've got a very good deal with management.

Cheers, Tilda.

PS It's not the same now you've gone. Too quiet.

Not that Lachlan was noisy, but his presence always made her feel more alive.

Lachlan pulled on clean clothes, threw his dirty scrubs into the theatre laundry basket and headed out to the car park to call Tilda. With a bit of luck she wouldn't be helping with an operation right now.

'Hi, Lachlan. How are you?'

Just hearing that chirpy voice sent tingles down his spine. 'I'm great. How's it going over there?'

'Much the same, busy, busy. You know how it is.'

So she wasn't missing him too much. Whereas he hadn't stopped thinking about her since he'd boarded the plane out of Phnom Penh.

'Everyone's pleased you're coming to work at Western General. Seems your reputation as being cool and calm in tricky situations has beaten you here.'

'Accepting the position was a no-brainer. Back in my home town and a great pay rate to boot.'

'So you're ready to settle here then?'

Say yes and we can have some fun together.

'Yes.'

He fist-pumped the air.

Tilda continued. 'Toronto was never going to be a permanent move. Nor anywhere else I might've ended up. I can't wait to find somewhere to live and unpack all the furniture and other gear I've got in storage. Could do with some different clothes too. Kind of tired of what I brought over here.'

'You'll have friends and family to catch up with too, no doubt.' The silence was suddenly deafening. 'Tilda? Did I put my size ten in it?'

'Not really. I don't have any family. My grandmother brought me up as my mother died in childbirth. Having me.' Her voice was low and sad. 'She never told anyone who my father was, and as she was an only child I don't have any relations that I know of.'

'I can't imagine what that's like.' There were times when his brother was a pain in the butt but he couldn't imagine not having him there to talk to and share a laugh whenever possible. Now that Ian lived in Quebec they mostly ribbed each other by phone.

'I'm used to it. My best friend and her fiancé live in Seattle. We met at school and have always been close.' A sigh came over the airwaves. 'Anyway, enough of that. Have the boys been pestering you?'

'Can't keep them away. They've heard about you and keep asking when you're coming to stay with me.'

'Really? You've already told everyone we're an item?'

'I bit the bullet at the weekend. Figured it would be easier for you if they'd already heard about our engagement before you arrived.' It hadn't been as hard to do as he'd expected.

'You might have to hold my hand through the meet-and-greets.'

'No problem. I like holding your hand.' He drew a breath. 'I'm missing you, Tilda. A lot. We got on so well it seems strange not having you around.' Maybe they could have a fling while she was here. He still wasn't sure he was ready to settle down again, but it seemed he was open to having a short-term relationship with her.

'Know what you mean. I miss not hanging out with you too.'

'I want to kiss you again.'

Her gasp came over the airwaves, sending a thrill of need down his spine. 'You do?'

'Of course I do. I can't stop thinking about those few kisses we shared and wanting more.'

A kissing sound reached him. 'Not quite the same, I know,' she said quietly. 'But I admit that it feels like I've been tossing and turning in frustration all night, every night. I can't get home soon enough.'

'Tell me something I don't know,' he growled.

Tilda put the phone down and hugged herself. *Tell me something I don't know*, he'd growled. That had to be the sexiest voice she'd heard him use yet. Lachlan wanted to kiss her some more. And she was desperate to kiss him back. And follow up with something more. Her hands itched to touch his body all over. To feel his pulse under her palm, his heat against her body, his sex between her fingers as she rubbed him. To hear that sexy voice talking to her, his lips caressing her skin.

Her fake fiancé was getting closer to her by the day, more so since he'd left here. As if being apart was a catalyst to needing to be together.

Picking up her phone, she scrolled through the numbers and tapped Lachlan's. 'Just wanted to say I'm dreaming of kissing you right now.'

'Tilda…' He groaned her name out, sending longing skyrocketing throughout her.

'Got to go. Talk again later.' She tossed the phone into her locker and headed into the ward to check up on a patient with a bounce in her step. It was strange how she and Lachlan seemed to be ratcheting up the tension and the desire to be together when they were so far apart. When he was here they'd kissed, and had begun to take tentative steps towards getting closer, but this was something else far more exciting. It was quite sudden how they were talking more intimately to each other, almost as though his leaving here had been what they'd both needed to see they cared for each other and wanted each other.

'When does your flight get in to Vancouver? I'll be there to pick you up,' Lachlan asked two days before she was due to leave Cambodia.

'I'll email you my ticket so you have the details.' Tilda sounded breathless. Keen to catch up?

He hoped so. There'd certainly been no hesitancy from her when they'd talked about kissing. He grunted a laugh. Their last phone conversation had been right on the edge of phone sex, only stopping when Tilda had heard someone call out for her.

'I'll be waiting for you.' No doubt impatiently.

He'd probably be at the airport waiting for her before her flight had even left the ground in Asia, he was so desperate to hold her in his arms. Almost from the moment he'd walked away from her at the charity centre he'd become more and more aware of how much he longed to have her in his bed. But that was getting ahead of things. So far they'd only kissed, and hinted at more, and yet now he couldn't imagine that not happening. His fake fiancée was coming home and he wanted nothing fake about their time together, however limited that might be.

'I'd better go. Dave's calling for me. Surgery's about to start.'

'See you on Saturday. Take care.'

'You too.' One of her squishy kiss sounds came through. 'Lachlan?'

'Yeah?'

'I can't wait to see you.' Click. She was gone.

Leaving his chest thumping and his head spinning with hope.

His finger moved fast over his phone screen.

Same back at you. xx

* * *

Lachlan stood outside the doors in the arrivals hall, tapping the floor with the tip of his shoe as he waited for Tilda. Two weeks never used to feel as long as the last two had. He'd been busy with work, and seeing the little guys and giving his house a lick and a polish for his guest, but each day had felt as though it lasted at least forty-eight hours long.

Where was she? Judging by the number of people coming out of Immigration, at least two planeloads of passengers must have disembarked since the arrival of her flight came up on the arrivals board.

His heart lifted. There she was, walking straight towards him with a wide smile on her beautiful face.

'You waiting for someone?' Her pack slid off her shoulder to land at her feet.

'You bet.' He wrapped her in his arms, making the most of that divine body pressed against him. Had he missed her, or what? Not quite how this was meant to pan out. Whatever *this* was.

Leaning back in his arms, her pelvis pressing into him was a reminder of how horny she made him feel with barely a touch. Then she looked up at him. That smile reached inside him to grab his heart so tightly he almost gasped out loud. Her hands were on his chest, making him just plain happy to be with her.

'Come here,' he groaned. His mouth found hers, and when she opened under his hungry lips he melted in an instant. 'I've missed you so much,' he murmured into her sweet, mint-flavoured mouth. Had she heard him? It was one thing to tell her over the phone, he discovered, but quite another to say it to her face.

Holding Tilda tighter, closer, he savoured her, his whole body smiling. She was home, with him, and he couldn't ask for anything more right at this moment.

Her mouth left his.

He leaned in to find hers again.

She tipped further back, her hands splayed wide on his chest now. 'Lachlan.' His name was rough and sexy on her tongue.

'Yes?'

The blue topaz of her eyes shone at him. 'I missed you too.'

She had heard him. Or was she reading him too easily? That was something she was very skilled at. From the moment she'd walked out of Immigration he hadn't tried to hide his feelings. He'd been too overwhelmed with the excitement of being with her to be able to cover his emotions.

'Let's go home. I think we've put on enough of a show for everyone here.'

Her laugh made him even harder. 'You think?'

Bending down to pick up her pack, he tweaked his trousers, then slung the pack over one arm so it fell in front of him. With his other hand he reached for Tilda's. 'Your ride awaits.'

'Not in a tuk-tuk, I hope.' Her smile further ramped up the need in him.

'Don't tell me you've already had enough of those?'

'I never really felt comfortable in them after my first experience. Kiry took me and Sally to town in his brand-new tuk-tuk one day as a way of saying thank you for chipping in to buy it, and I couldn't relax entirely. He still had his lower leg in a cast!'

'Everyone put money towards it.' Kiry was popular with the staff and, as Lachlan had expected, they'd refused to hear of him buying it for the man on his own. Something he'd totally understood because he'd have done the same if another person had come up with the idea. 'Has he been giving them all free rides?'

'Each and every one of the staff. I had to take a second ride for you. Kiry said we were in the accident together, we should have to ride together, and since you weren't there I got two goes.' Tilda shivered. 'I chose somewhere very close to the hospital for the second one.'

Lachlan leaned in and brushed a kiss on her cheek. 'I owe you.'

Her finger ran along his bottom lip. 'I'll take it out of your hide. It hasn't been the same since you left. Not for me anyway. The one highlight was seeing little Phala pretty much fully recovered.'

He grinned. 'I bet. I'm thrilled the little guy is better.' He was glad to hear how much she'd missed him too. Somehow, it gave him the confidence to go forward with their plan. 'Let's get out of here.'

Her smile widened into a full-blown hello, great to see you look.

Did this mean they would continue having a great time together for a little while? Have a fling of epic portions? Or risk becoming more involved?

Digging a bigger hole to get out of when our time is inevitably up, warned the sensible side of his brain.

Even if it only ended up being a fling, it would still be devastating when it ended, he suspected. But right at this moment it seemed he couldn't care less. He was so glad to see Tilda and to be able to touch her, hear her laugh and chatter away happily. Tomorrow was another day for the worries to resurface.

As they headed into the city Tilda said, 'Thanks for the upgrade to first class. I had the best sleep I've ever had on a plane. Couldn't complain about the service either,' she said with a laugh.

'Guess that means you won't be falling asleep as soon as we get home.'

She faked a yawn. 'Want to bet?'

His fingers drummed on the steering wheel as an image of Tilda in his bed filled his head.

Whoa. Slow down.

But hell, he'd missed her so much more than he'd have believed possible. He wanted her. In all ways possible.

Again, slow down.

They had to be so, so careful.

Tilda breathed deep, relishing the scent that was Lachlan. Bumps rose on her forearms and her fingers tightened as she fought the urge to reach over and grip his thigh, to feel his heat under her hand. He might pull over and leave her on the side of the road if she did that, although after their last few phone conversations and the welcome she'd received at the airport she somehow doubted it.

When he'd hauled her into his arms and

kissed her senseless when she'd walked up to him in the terminal she'd known where she wanted this to go. And suspected he felt much the same. He'd got horny—fast. Yes, she'd noticed. Hard not to. She laughed at the corny pun. Hard. Yep. He wanted her all right. She wanted him too. All caution seemed to have been hurled to the wind.

His thigh was tense under her palm.

She pressed it a little harder. Her fingers clung to the taut muscles. Her mouth dried while her heart rate hit the roof.

How far was it to his house? She knew how to get to his suburb but had no idea how long it took. Only that it would be too long. A tense, teasing, long time.

Lachlan gently lifted her hand away and placed it back on her lap. 'I've got to concentrate.' His voice came out all husky and low and upped the level of heat in her core to what felt like volcanic proportions. It was nothing like she'd heard from any man before.

'Sorry.' She wasn't really. He hadn't thrown her out of the car. She was only sorry it was taking for ever to get wherever they were going.

'Don't be.' He leaned forward as though to focus on the road and ignore her. But then he gave her a quick glance and that beautiful mouth curved into the most tempting smile, and she relaxed.

A little. Not so much that the pounding in her chest disappeared, but she could sit back and watch him as he drove. As long as he broke every speed limit on the way.

What had happened to change everything so fast? When they'd kissed before she'd wanted him, but not like this. Not with the feeling that if she didn't have him she'd shatter into a million little pieces. Two weeks without seeing Lachlan, only hearing him talking in that low, nerve-tingling voice, and she'd been hot for him the whole time. Then the moment she'd set eyes on him again today she was completely lost. It was something to think about, but not now. That would be impossible. Thinking of anything sensible at all seemed beyond her.

If only she could touch his stubble with her fingertips. But the last thing she needed was to distract him and be in another car accident.

It was going to be strange walking into his home as his fiancée, staying until she found a place for herself, though she supposed that might change in the short-term if they started a fling. When Lachlan had gone home she'd begun to realise just how badly she wanted him. The worry that she might be making a big mistake still remained, as did the concern that he might hurt her more the deeper in she got. Yet not seeing him every day had been pure torture.

What did he feel about her? Before he'd left Cambodia he'd told her he wasn't interested in getting into a relationship. She'd said much the same in reply. She'd meant it and still felt that way. They might be hot for each other, but that was a whole different ball game to thinking about anything permanent. Apart from kisses and sex, because sex was foremost in her head at the moment. She wasn't ready for anything more.

But, whatever played out between them, she had a role to play in his life at the moment. For the first time she wondered if she'd taken on more than she could deal with by pretending to be engaged to him. The ending could hurt if she let these new feelings of want for him take over. So the sensible answer was to keep the brakes in place and enjoy whatever unfolded slowly. She could stand up and be accountable for her own needs while giving back something to the man who'd inspired these feelings in her. Starting with making love. Yeah, well, if he didn't hurry up, she was going to explode with need before they got to his house.

Finally, when it felt as though she was just about to expire from sheer frustration, Lach-

Ian turned into a driveway and drove up into a garage, barely waiting for the door to lift high enough to go under.

He pressed a control hanging from the sun visor to close the garage behind them. As he braked and turned the engine off he was already reaching for her to start kissing her hard and deep. How had he managed to drive with all that passion simmering in his veins?

Glad they'd made it, she kissed him back without reservation. This was what she'd been looking for, wanting so badly.

'Tilda, we'd better get out of the car before one of us gets bruised.' The gear stick was digging into his thigh.

Her seatbelt was uncomfortably hard against her breasts. Without pulling her mouth away she felt behind her for the door handle, then opened the door and abruptly jerked upright. 'Come on.'

They met again at the front of the car, eyes only for each other, hands reaching out. Then Lachlan was grabbing one of hers and racing her through the internal door into the house, where he headed for the sweeping staircase.

They were all but running. Tilda held his hand tight, not wanting to lose touch with him for a second.

'In here,' he gasped at the top of the stairs

as he turned them into a big room with a massive bed beckoning.

'Pinch me,' she whispered as she slowed. She'd never seen a bed so big.

'Let's go for a kiss instead.' Lachlan was already holding her face gently and lowering his mouth to hers.

'Any time you like,' she replied softly, before stretching up to wind her arms around his neck and hold on. Her legs were running out of strength as desire soared through her, and the last thing she wanted was to land on her butt on the floor. 'Lachlan.' She breathed his name slowly.

'Tilda, slow down. You're winding me up so tight I'm going to lose control and it'll all be over in a minute. And that's the last thing I want.'

He scooped her up in his arms and turned for the bed, where he laid her down with excruciating slowness, kissing her neck and driving her insane with need for him.

'Lachlan,' she gasped through a haze of longing. Her fingers were clumsy as she worked on the buttons in front of her, trying to focus so she could last longer than a few seconds. Her body was crying out for him, for release with him inside her.

'Let me.' He tugged his shirt over his head

and tossed it aside, exposing the wide muscular chest she'd only felt under her palms and through his shirt when they'd kissed before. She traced his muscles, feeling his hot skin, wanting, wanting, wanting more.

'Can I remove your blouse?' His voice was husky with passion, his eyes dark with lust.

She pushed up and began to pull her top over her head.

'I'll help…' His hands replaced hers on the blouse and as he removed it he leaned in to place a line of kisses from her waist up to her ribs, to first one breast, then the other.

She was crying out with the sweetness and the agony of it all. Bring it on. 'I can't last, Lachlan.'

'Yes, you can.' Fingers flicked her nipples, and then his mouth headed south, licking, kissing, over her stomach and on down to her womanhood. Her legs trembled and her hands were fists at her sides and her back was arching upward in agonised ecstasy.

'Take me, Lachlan. Now. Please,' she begged.

He replied with a hard stroke of his tongue.

She shuddered. Unable to wait any longer, she slipped under his body and exhaled with the thrill of his weight on top of her, the feel of his blood pounding through his veins.

'No, Tilda. Let me bring you to the brink first.'

'I'm already there.' She moved her hand down his hot, hard length and then squeezed him gently.

His eyes widened, his face tensed and then he gasped, 'Hang on. Condoms are on the bedside table.'

Oh, yes. Rolling a condom down that hard shaft was as good as anything so far, her fingers played with him, teasing all the way.

Then he was taking her hands away and plunging deep inside her, pulling back to push in gloriously again, and again.

Tilda's body tightened as waves of desire rocketed between them, and she cried out as she shattered into a million pieces. She also felt whole again for the first time in a long time.

'Where is she?' Lachlan's mother strode into the kitchen an hour later, his father right on her heels. 'I want to meet this woman who's put a smile on my son's face.'

'Tilda's having a shower, Mum.' Sometimes he wished they didn't have an open home policy where the family came and went as they pleased. To be fair, there'd never been an issue before, but what if his parents had turned up thirty minutes ago? That would've been awkward.

His mother walked over to the door and tilted her head as though listening to something. Then she smiled again. 'Your en suite shower, by the sound of it. You haven't wasted any time, then.'

I'm thirty-seven, damn it, he thought moodily. *Not a kid needing supervision.*

'We'll see,' he muttered. He wasn't quite sure where he and Tilda were at after that mind-blowing sex. It couldn't be a one-off. No, it wouldn't. From her response, there'd surely be a lot more where that came from.

His mother walked past, patting him on the arm. 'I'll make some coffee while we wait.'

He should've warned Tilda his mother could be a bit OTT when it came to her son, and now he was supposedly engaged she wouldn't be quiet about it. Apparently, he'd never stopped smiling since arriving back from Cambodia, which had her overly excited. He felt his mother was exaggerating. He admitted he was happier than he'd been when he'd left to go to the charity hospital, but hardly enough to suggest anything deep and meaningful was happening here just yet. Only great sex. But there was some truth in the fact Tilda had changed him and made him see there could possibly be a future for him at some point that involved love, and even a family, even if it wasn't with her.

Big step there, Lachlan.

True. The fear of losing another loved one still gripped him when he wasn't being careful. So slowly, slowly was the only way to go. How about going back to bed with Tilda—after he'd sent his parents packing and locked the doors?

Need to change the locks for that to work.

'See? He's daydreaming again,' his mother said with a laugh.

'Give the man a break,' his father grunted. 'He doesn't need his mother interfering in his love life.' He winked at Lachlan.

'Oh, hello.' Tilda stood in the doorway, looking hesitant.

'Hey, Tilda, these are my parents, Faye and John.' He crossed to be with her, to show solidarity. After all, Tilda had come up with the fiancée idea to support him.

'Hello, Tilda, nice to meet you.' His mother gave her a quick hug before stepping back, sussing out the woman before her. 'This is a bit of a surprise for all of us, I have to say.'

Tilda blinked, then smiled, looking almost at ease. 'For both of us too.' She turned to his dad and held out her hand. 'Hello, John.'

'Welcome home,' his dad said with a cheeky smile.

Parents. Lachlan grimaced. Had he really been such a sad sack for so long that these two were so desperate to see him happy again they'd go along with anything he did? It had been devastating losing Kelly, and then Matt, but surely he'd managed a few laughs in the intervening time?

'It's been a bit sudden, you two meeting and getting engaged,' his mother commented pointedly.

'We first met a year ago,' Lachlan said to throw her off the scent.

'You did?'

Tilda blinked, then straightened her shoulders. 'Yes, but I've been working in Toronto for a lot of that year.'

'I see.' It was obvious his mum didn't, because he'd never mentioned Tilda before returning from Cambodia. No reason to when he hadn't expected to meet her again.

'How do you like your coffee, Tilda?' his mother asked.

'White, no sugar, thanks.'

'I hear you're starting work at Western General this week,' John said. 'You're going to be in the same area of the hospital as Lachlan.'

'Small world, isn't it? But then I think Lach-

Ian might have had some influence there, though he's denying it, of course.'

Lachlan shrugged. 'The department's been looking for a really top-notch theatre nurse for a while. There's a nationwide shortage at the moment.'

'Top-notch, eh?' His father grinned.

This was getting worse by the minute. 'Mum, Dad, back off, will you? At this rate you'll scare Tilda away.'

His mother passed Tilda a mug of coffee. 'I see you haven't got an engagement ring yet.'

Another blink from Tilda. 'We'll get around to that once I've settled in here and at work. There's no hurry.' She gave him a desperate look.

It was only supposed to be a temporary situation. Why would they have thought about getting a ring?

'That's something we'll do when we're ready. It's meant to be a special time and I'm not dragging Tilda to the jeweller's while she's still getting over jet lag and unpacking her belongings from the storage unit she's using.' Lachlan put an arm around Tilda's shoulders and drew her closer.

His mother smiled softly. 'You could wear Lachlan's grandmother's ring in the meantime, Tilda. It's a diamond solitaire. Quite beautiful, and it needs to come out of the box where it's lain for a few years.'

Tilda tensed a fraction. 'Um…thank you, but that won't be necessary.'

'My family do like to interfere in my life,' he told her with a tight laugh. 'We'll talk about it later, Mum.'

Tilda looked up at him and smiled. 'It's okay. I understand they want you to be happy.'

'We do,' his mum agreed. 'It's been a long stretch since he was, and so it's natural to think you are the cause of those smiles.'

His father cleared his throat. 'We'd love you to come to the charity lunch we're putting on at our home in a fortnight, Tilda. No doubt Lachlan would be bringing you anyway, but I'm making it an official invite. We do this once a year to raise funds for children with leukaemia. I'm a pathologist, by the way.'

'Hence the charity.' Tilda nodded. Her shoulders lifted as she drew a breath. 'Thank you for the invitation. I'd love to come, though I'll need to find a suitable outfit. I take it this won't be a casual affair?'

Not within an inch.

'We'll talk about that later too.' Next thing, his mother would be offering to take her shopping and that might lead to more problems. His mother's idea of where to shop for clothes was nothing like what he'd seen of Tilda's wardrobe so far. But then she might have a load of expensive outfits in that lockup where her things were stored. There were still a lot of things he didn't know about this wonderful woman. But he was going to enjoy finding out, if his parents didn't scare her off first.

His mother opened her mouth.

He shook his head warningly at her.

She closed her mouth and went back to making coffee for the rest of them.

What have I walked into? Tilda asked herself as she looked around the expansive kitchen and dining area. The house was massive, and furnished beautifully. There was real money behind Lachlan, something she hadn't even considered. Why would she? It wasn't on her radar when meeting people.

'It won't be difficult to stay out of your way, Lachlan,' she teased in an attempt to gain some control over her mixed-up feelings about where she was and what they were doing.

'Why would you want to do that?' he teased.

She had walked out of Immigration and into his arms like they were an item. They had gone straight to his bed when they'd arrived here.

'You know. Those days when you're way too busy and feeling grumpy and everyone's a nuisance.' Not that she'd seen one of those days affect him yet. She was talking for the sake of it.

His mother might be making coffee but her ears were like revolving radar, picking up every word and nuance. Best keep calm and steady, try to forget how her feelings for the woman's son were erupting all over the place.

Lachlan grinned. 'Haven't got time for those.' Then he added, 'I do rattle around in here. It's better when the boys come round. Though they like hiding and it takes for ever to find them. Or it would if they ever stopped giggling.'

'They're still at the giggling age? Love it.' Starting tomorrow, she'd get to know the boys a little. How many weeks would she have here? She should get onto finding an apartment ASAP, but it was hard to get excited about that at the moment. After making love with Lachlan, the only place she wanted to be was in this house where that large bed beckoned. His lovemaking had been a game-changer. Before, she'd thought a fling would be exciting. Now she wanted more where that came from, along with getting to know him in so many more ways.

'Campbell, the oldest lad, likes to think he's too old for little boys' games, but that doesn't stop him partaking if there's an ice cream at the end of it,' Faye was telling her.

'Kids, eh?' Strange how the longing for one of her own had started growing since Lachlan became part of her life. It couldn't be because her body clock was ticking down. There were years to go. She was thirty, not forty. Plenty of time to get her life running smoothly before doing something about finding a surrogate father—if she didn't go and fall in love. A sideways glance at Lachlan had her straightening up and moving to put a small gap between them. It would be all too easy to hand her heart over to him if she wasn't very careful. But he'd never indicated he was open to anything but a temporary fling.

Both John and Faye were looking at her with something like hope in their eyes. What had happened to them wanting Lachlan to marry Meredith? Was it just that they really wanted him to be happy and it didn't matter who that was with?

This was crazy. She wasn't their son's partner, and suddenly the lie was becoming overwhelming. Gulp.

'I'm sure Lachlan has lots of ice cream in that freezer just waiting for the boys.' She nodded to the upright freezer by what she presumed was the butler's pantry.

'Every flavour you can imagine,' he answered with something like relief in his voice. So he'd sensed her unease and was hoping she'd keep quiet about the truth?

Putting her coffee mug down, Tilda faked a yawn. 'Sorry, but the flight's catching up with me.'

Suddenly everyone was busy drinking coffee. Lachlan gave her a small smile, knowing what she'd done and thankfully wasn't cross with her.

'Right, we'd better be going. I need to drop by the garden centre,' John said.

Faye gave Tilda a hug. 'It's lovely to meet you,' Lachlan's mother said quietly. 'I mean that, even though we've been taken by surprise at how quickly you two have got together.'

'I understand.'

More than you know.

Okay, she and Lachlan needed to have a talk about dealing with this, because she clearly hadn't thought it through properly when she'd made the offer to be his fiancée, but right now that was the last thing she felt like doing. She *was* suddenly very tired. Hardly surprising given the long flight and then making energetic love with Lachlan. Right now she wanted quiet time with him and no one else. No discussions about a pretend relationship. No talk about outfits for a glamorous luncheon. Only time to absorb where she was, and who she was with, and how well their bodies had reacted to each other.

'I'm sorry everything's suddenly caught up with me.'

'You get some sleep and I'll see you again before the luncheon.'

'Mum means she'll be around here early in the week, if not tomorrow,' Lachlan told her after his parents had left. 'She likes to be in charge.'

'I hate that we'll eventually disappoint her.'

'That'll be for me to deal with.'

'Still, it won't be easy. She's being so kind to me.'

'I bet she turns up with the boys tomorrow. It will be an excuse to talk to you some more.'

'I can't wait to meet the little guys.' But as for his mother? That was tricky because she already liked Faye. The woman was warm and caring, and very open. Yes, Tilda was happy to see more of her, as long as she wasn't too intent on sussing her out about every last little thing.

Looking at Lachlan, her heart lurched. He was awesome, and she was starting to care for him, despite her own warnings. Another surprise was how much she wanted to see Lachlan playing with the boys. She'd bet he was a great father figure to them. Another side to him that would only make her admire him that bit more.

'Bet they're adorable.'

'They are. Two of them are so like Matt, it freaks me out sometimes.'

'It must be wonderful having children and watching them grow up.' Damn. 'Sorry, that came out wrong.'

'Because Matt won't see his boys become young men? Don't apologise. You're being normal and, to be honest, I'm tired of people tiptoeing around the fact he's gone.' He'd watched her closely as they'd talked about the boys. 'You didn't think of having children when you were married?'

As much as she didn't like talking about herself or her past, if they were going to become closer then she had to be completely honest about everything so there'd be no comebacks later if anything went pear-shaped. 'I fell pregnant once. It wasn't planned but I was so excited. It made me realise how much I wanted to have a complete family.' She stood beside Lachlan, looking out across the front lawn. Kids would love playing here. 'Then I lost the baby.'

His arms wrapped around her. 'That's awful. How did you cope?' He breathed the question against her neck.

For a distraction it wasn't bad, but she needed to finish this conversation. 'It wasn't easy as I was devastated. But the worst part was that James was pleased. He didn't want a baby in our lives. It would mean he didn't get all my attention.' She hugged Lachlan back and then stepped out of his arms. 'I really am better off without him.'

'I agree. Never liked him from the moment he started shouting at you in hospital.'

As far as she knew, it was the only time he'd ever seen James. But his support had surprised her. So unlike anything James would've done.

She looked around, taking in what she could see of the house from here. The kitchen was state-of-the-art with white walls, tiles and benches. Everything shone enough to blind her if she stared too hard. 'Are you into cooking?'

'My thing's strictly heating up take-outs,' he said, laughing. Then stopped and turned to take her hands in his. 'Welcome to my house, Tilda. Make yourself completely at home with everything. I want you to be happy here.'

That wouldn't be hard. 'From what I've seen of it so far, you have a lovely home.' She spun around and gazed out of the big windows onto another large lawn edged with perfectly laid flowerbeds. 'Who looks after all that?'

'I have a gardener and a cleaner for inside

the house, in case you think I might put you on cleaning duties.'

'I wouldn't know where to start.' Her apartments were usually boxes with one bedroom and no space to swing a cat. Crikey, not once had she considered Lachlan might be this well-off. It didn't make a bit of difference to how she felt about him, but it still came as a bit of a shock. Should've realised when she saw his top-of-the-range car at the airport. And the upgrade to first class for her flight home. That had been special.

'Here, take a pew.' He pulled a stool out from under the counter. 'I'll get another coffee on the go.'

Elbows on the counter, chin in her hands, she watched him and for the first time since she'd walked out of Immigration into his hug she truly relaxed. First the build-up of need that had pulsed between them all the way from the airport to his bed, and then his parents arriving and keeping her on her toes with their ideas about their relationship. No wonder she'd got a bit tense. Now, sitting here as though she'd always been here felt good. She'd got wound up on the flight home, thinking about where they were at and if there might be any awkwardness between them after two weeks apart. She didn't want that. Lachlan was easy-going, not into making demands of her. Yet.

He won't. But… *He could.* So much for relaxing.

'How's work been since you got back?'

'Great. I have felt different since Cambodia. Felt more comfortable from the moment I got away from here, really. Now I look forward to going into work every morning, and when the boys come around I join their games without worrying if I'm doing the right thing by them and hoping Matt would be happy about how I look out for them. I've been to dinner with Mum and Dad twice since I got back. We've talked about Matt, and Kelly, and the road trip they're planning. I've also made it clear I'm moving on, so when I mentioned this woman I met again in Phnom Penh I figure they thought she was the reason I'm suddenly coming to terms with the past and am now looking forward. The engagement knocked them sideways, but they've taken it on board quite quickly.'

'And Meredith?'

'She was stunned at first, but has since told me she'll back me in whatever I do. Says she's trying to sort her life out too, and that maybe she'd pressured me too much.'

'That's exactly what you wanted to hear

from her. Now you—we—just have to keep this going for a bit longer, and not get side-tracked.'

'You're definitely part of why I am where I am now.' Lachlan came over and took her hands in his. 'I'd like to spend more time with you, get to know you a little better. What do you think?' He was grinning in that way that went straight to her knees and made her legs useless at holding her upright. Just as well she was sitting down.

'I think we're on the same page.'

His grin got bigger. 'The relief is enormous.'

He wasn't trying to control her. Big point in his favour. Standing up, she hooked her hands around his neck. 'What say we go back to your bedroom?' she asked.

'Don't you mean *our* bedroom, fake fiancée?'

CHAPTER SEVEN

'LACHLAN, WHERE ARE YOU?' a boy shouted from the back door. 'We've brought the new soccer ball to play with.'

Lachlan grinned. 'Here we go. Your peace and quiet is over for the morning.'

Tilda looked up from her laptop on the counter. 'You, playing soccer? This I must watch.'

'Not good enough. You've got to join in too. Ground rules. Everyone here has to play the game that's happening.'

Faye burst into the room. 'Hello, Lachlan, Tilda.'

Lachlan gave Tilda an apologetic look. 'See you outside shortly.'

Thanks. Leave me with your mum and her questions, why don't you?

'Morning, Faye. Come to play soccer, have you?'

'Me? Not likely.' Faye sat at the table opposite Tilda, giving her the uncomfortable feeling she was in for an inquisition. 'I'm more the sideline ref type.'

'Isn't that true.' Another woman joined them. Tilda recognised her immediately from the photo on Lachlan's phone.

'Tilda, this is Meredith, the boys' mother. Meredith, meet the woman who's got Lachlan twisted around her little finger and making him smile every day.'

Tilda looked around for Lachlan but he was nowhere in sight. Had he heard that last comment? He surely wouldn't have walked away if he had. Would he? No, she didn't believe he'd leave her in the lurch with his mother and the woman who'd wanted him to marry her. But then she could be too trusting when it came to men she cared for.

'Hi, Meredith. I'm Tilda, and no, I am not responsible for *all* Lachlan's smiles.' She wanted to downplay all this as it made her somewhat uneasy.

'Actually, you caused a fair few of them,' said Lachlan from the doorway. He grinned at her wickedly.

He hadn't abandoned her after all. But what he'd just said only added to the pressure of trying to keep everything as open and honest as she could without blowing the cover on what she was doing for him. Raising one eyebrow

in his direction, she said, 'Go and play soccer.'
They'd talk later when no one else was around
to suck up every word and rearrange them to
suit their own wishes.

'On my way. Meredith, I need some adult
support out here.'

The boys' mother shook her head. 'Like you
can't manage my three all by yourself.' But she
stood up. 'It's good to meet you after hearing
all about you these past couple of weeks. And
yes, he does seem happier.'

Tilda could feel her face reddening. This
was way more than she'd expected when she'd
offered to stand beside Lachlan against his
family's pressure to remarry. Somehow she'd
thought she'd just be in the background. Silly
girl.

'Spending time working in such a different environment probably has something to
do with that too. I found Cambodia stimulat-
ing myself.'

Meredith smiled knowingly. 'I can see that's
what's happened to Lachlan.' Then she headed
outside.

Faye pulled out a chair and sat down opposite Tilda.

*Here we go. She's not going to let me off the
hook so easily. Best get in first and cut her off
at the pass.*

'Faye, I understand you want Lachlan to be happy and find love again, but that our engagement has come as a shock to you all.'

'We weren't expecting it, that's for sure. Didn't even know he'd met someone. But if he's happy then so are we.'

'I think I understand.'

'Tell me a little about yourself. If you don't mind, that is.'

'Of course not.' It was normal to want to know about the woman her son had got engaged to.

'Are you a Vancouverite born and bred?'

The tightness in her gut eased a fraction. She could answer these sorts of questions, even when she usually avoided them. It might help Faye accept Lachlan was moving on in his own way.

'Yes. My grandmother brought me up in the eastern suburbs.'

'No mother?'

'She died in childbirth.'

A soft, warm hand covered hers. 'I'm sorry, Tilda. That must've been hard living with, growing up.'

'It was. But Grandma was the strongest, most loving woman I could've wanted. I didn't miss out on the basics either.' She still missed her, and always would.

'I suppose our family and how we all tumble through each other's lives must seem daunting to you. Even Meredith and her lads are part of the scene. Her family's always been friends with ours, and Matt hung around with Lachlan since they were teens.' Faye sat back. 'We all sort of slot together, if you know what I mean.'

'Lachlan's mentioned that. He's so lucky in that way. He also told me about Kelly.'

'It was a huge shock for all of us, but especially Lachlan. He was devastated.'

'I can't begin to imagine what he's been through. Then to lose his best friend as well.' Okay, it was time to tell Faye some of her history. 'I was married but I left my ex a little more than a year ago, after I was in a serious car accident and he was more upset about the car than me. He was a bully and I'd had enough.'

'Sounds like you're a strong woman.'

'I try to be.'

'Divorced?'

'It's in the pipeline.'

'Thank you for telling me this. It helps to know a little more about you.' She stood up. 'Let's go and watch the boys playing.'

'Faye, I understand you need time to absorb the fact Lachlan's moving on without your help, but believe me, he is happier than he was previously.'

Not necessarily because of her, though she hoped she was helping. He was always cheerful when he was with her. He also ticked a lot of her own boxes when it came to a man she wanted to spend time with.

For a moment the smile faded from the older woman's eyes. Sudden sorrow for her struck Tilda. All Faye wanted was for her son to be happy, but her idea of how that would happen hadn't come to fruition.

I want it to happen too—but his way, not yours.

'Let things take their course.' Whichever way that went. The same could be said for herself. Wait and see how this new—fake—relationship unfolded. She wanted to be with Lachlan and find out if they were starting out on a new adventure or if the fling they'd engaged in was all there was to be had.

'You're right. It's just that I feel rather useless. I'm his mother, and I haven't been able to fix everything for him.'

'He's getting there.'

'He and Kelly had something very special and losing her took the ground right out from under him. I only want him to be just as happy again.'

Tilda reached across and took her hands. 'He knows that. He also worries for all of you, but

I think he's looking forwards now.' She didn't know him as well as these people but he was strong and focused and ready to go after what he wanted. A small piece of her heart would like to become a part of that, but she was still wary of it being too much, too soon.

'Thank you, Tilda.'

'Come on. Let's see how the game's going.'

Outside, the boys were chasing Lachlan around the lawn as much as they were the ball. 'Their energy levels are high. I wonder how long Lachlan will last?' Tilda said aloud, knowing how much energy he'd used *playing* with her that morning.

Meredith laughed. 'He's good at this. They think they're winning, but Lachlan's in charge.'

He was having fun, no doubt about it. Shouting and laughing as loudly as the boys as he dashed up and down, kicking the ball whenever it wasn't too close to anyone. Tilda watched with a growing sense of longing. Family. Standing here, it seemed so simple. A ball, three boys and Lachlan, their mum and Faye— and herself—watching and enjoying. Family. She'd watched her school mates' families from the outside, dreaming of sharing noisy meals and arguments over whose turn it was to set the table or feed the dog, looking out for each other when other kids tried to pick fights with them. Growing up with Grandma had been safe and loving, but awfully lonely at times.

Yet today it all seemed so easy. These people had it sorted. Of course, that wasn't right. The boys didn't have a father any more. Their mother was struggling with getting on with her life. But Tilda would swear they were happy in their own ways.

Can I have this?

She could if she put aside her fear of making the same mistake she had with James and allowed herself to fall head over heels in love with Lachlan. Getting ahead of herself, surely? Maybe, but, for the first time, she wasn't about to run from the idea either.

He looked her way and smiled that big smile of his that curled her toes and set her heart racing. Did he have ESP? Was he telling her yes, she could have it all? With him? Not likely.

'You have changed him,' Meredith said quietly. 'There's a new calmness about him I haven't seen in for ever.'

That probably had little to do with her, given they hadn't known each other for much more than four weeks, even if they did meet a year ago.

'It's been a long time for him, hasn't it?' These people were so open about things, they made it too easy for her to respond in a like manner.

'Yes. Sometimes I wondered if he'd ever get over losing Kelly. Then I lost Matt, and now I totally understand.'

'Lachlan said you've met a man you like.' Going too far? Even when Meredith seemed so open. They'd barely met, after all.

'We've been out for coffee a few times. He's nice, but I'm not sure if he's the right man for me. You know what I mean? I've got kids to think of, and I'm afraid of falling for someone and losing them again.'

Did anyone come without baggage?

'Take your time, Meredith.'

Says the expert here.

'Have some fun, and enjoy yourself first. Getting back out there onto the dating scene is scary.'

'It's worked for you.' When Tilda turned to look at her, she added, 'Yes, Lachlan did tell me you'd been married and that you'd left your husband last year.'

Did that mean he cared enough he wanted those close to him to accept her in his life as more than a *fake* fiancée? She couldn't see him talking up the engagement too much when they were meant to call it off later if he wasn't at least thinking they might have something going between them. Or was she just projecting her own desires onto him?

When Tilda didn't reply, Meredith added hurriedly, 'It's okay. He was only explaining why you didn't have your own place to return to. He wasn't filling me in on all the personal details, only that it seemed right for you to move in with him. Lachlan doesn't do tell-all. Especially about a woman he's keen on.'

Tilda felt her face warm. She'd been so thrilled when Lachlan took her to bed the first time, pleased he might have some feelings for her, even if only desire, but now Meredith—and Faye—seemed to think he was truly invested in her, which was the plan, but in reality was scary. They were lying to his lovely family and it had been her idea.

She returned to the original topic. 'Go on another date, and just enjoy it. Don't question every minute of your time with this guy who has got you wondering what lies ahead.'

'Did Lachlan tell you I'd hoped that he and I might eventually get together?'

Tilda nodded. 'He did.'

'He was right to push me away. We've always been close friends, but the X-factor never existed between us. Settling down with him would've been an easy way out of my difficulties. We would've regretted it long-term, I know that.'

'And possibly lost a close friend along the way.'

'True,' Meredith agreed. 'Thanks for listening to me. I can see why Lachlan cares for you. I hope we get to spend more time together. That's when he's not monopolising you.'

'When's the coffee break?' Lachlan appeared in front of her, understanding in his eyes. Had he overheard them talking?

'I'll go and make it now,' Meredith offered and walked off.

His hand was hot on her arm, and he leaned close so only she heard him. 'It's okay. We'll ride this out. Promise.'

'I'm feeling a little guilty.'

'I get that too. Let's give it time. Give ourselves time. Who knows? We might find we want more than a quick fling together.'

Her heart lifted. They appeared to be on the same path, wherever that might lead.

'I'll go and help Meredith with the coffee.' *And get my breath back.*

Lachlan brushed a light kiss on her mouth. 'Can you bring out some lemonade for the boys too? That'll win them over in a flash.'

* * *

'Scalpel.' Lachlan held out his hand.

Tilda obliged by placing the instrument in his hand, grinning at the command. Because, yes, in Theatre Lachlan could be curt because he was focused entirely on the job and nothing, nobody, would deflect him unless there was a problem with his patient's vitals.

'I'm making an incision around the nipple.' A breast reduction coming up.

'Can you do anything to hide those grooves in Annabel's shoulders?' she asked as she watched every move he made. The weight of their fifty-year-old patient's breasts had caused a deep trough-like hollow on her shoulders where her bra straps sat.

He was so precise as he made the cuts ready to remove excess tissue and fat from the breast. 'I can't fill them in, so no. Physio and massage therapy will ease the aching but that's the best we can do. She will feel less and less aching as time goes on.' He nodded at the right breast. 'Clean that area.'

Tilda swabbed beneath the incision, then changed swabs in preparation for more bleeding as Lachlan continued.

It was Friday and the first time she'd worked alongside him at Western G. Wednesday had been mostly an orientation day, and then yesterday she'd been rostered in Theatre One while he'd been operating in Theatre Three. They'd crossed paths in the tea room once, and had to wait until they got home to catch up on each other's day over a glass of wine. It had felt cosy in a way she hadn't known since she was a kid and talking to Grandma about her day at school.

'Do you give your patients a choice on the size their breasts are reduced to?'

'Of course. It's not my place to say what they should have, though I do point out the pluses and negatives of going too small. Or too large.'

'I hadn't worked with plastic surgeons before Phnom Penh.'

'Nothing different to other surgeries for us,' the other nurse on this case said.

'I guess you're right,' Tilda agreed. 'But it's interesting. I like that Lachlan's making people feel better about themselves, not only pain-wise but visually. So many have hang-ups about their looks, it's like a circus out there sometimes. Too big, too little, ugly, beautiful. The list goes on and on. It's crazy.'

'You're not wrong there,' Lachlan said. 'Right, I need to see how I'm doing for size. We're aiming for a twelve.' Lachlan spoke to the room generally.

Tilda handed him the measure. And squeezed

her shoulders together. Just the thought of having a surgeon cutting into her breasts made her eyes water. She was lucky hers were average-sized. Lachlan seemed to like them, though.

Behave, Tilda. That's out of place.

Yeah, but he was so hot, even dressed in the ghastly blue work garb that did nothing to highlight the amazing body underneath.

'Looking good. The first one's the easiest, it's making the second match as perfectly as possible that takes more time.' His brow creased as he concentrated on the second breast.

'Heart rate's dropping.' The anaesthetist spoke across everyone. 'Fifty-five.'

'What's up, Jeremy?' Lachlan asked, his hands suddenly still. 'Bradycardia?'

'I'd say so. I'm administering five milligrams of ephedrine.'

'I'll keep going until you say otherwise. Can't leave her like this.'

Tilda swabbed regularly and handed Lachlan whatever he required as soon as he asked.

'Heart rate fifty-nine,' Jeremy reported.

Relief filtered through Lachlan's eyes as he concentrated on removing more tissue from the second breast. A lowered heart rate wasn't a physician's fault, but they always felt it was.

Tilda felt the same. Bradycardia wasn't uncommon but it still scared her to bits when it occurred with a patient she was nursing. People came into surgery nervous but trusting everyone to see them come out the other side better off than they went in.

Four hours after Annabel was wheeled into Theatre, Tilda rolled her bed out into Recovery. 'All done,' she said to Annabel, who was still out of it.

'Any problems?' asked the recovery nurse taking over.

'Yes.' Tilda filled her in. 'But Annabel came right as soon as the ephedrine was administered.' She rolled onto her toes and stretched upward to ease the kinks out of her back and shoulders.

'Go grab a coffee and something to eat.'

'Think I will. I'm on again this afternoon.' Not with Lachlan. Her next patient was in for a knee replacement.

'What have you got this afternoon?' she asked when he joined her on the way to the staff tea room.

'Eighteen-month-old with a cleft palate.' He picked up the bagel he'd bought. 'You like working here?'

'So far it's good. The staff all seem friendly.'

'Aren't they in every theatre?'

'Mostly.' She wasn't going to tell him that

some surgeons could be a bit up themselves. This one certainly wasn't. 'What time do you reckon you'll be finished?'

'That's like asking what the weather's going to be like in a month's time.' He grinned.

'Want to go out for something to eat tonight? Since I can't cook to save myself and it is my turn to put food on the table. My shout,' she added, in case he thought she was taking advantage of his generous nature.

'You're on. I'll text when I'm leaving for home. Got any idea where you want to go?'

'What's that bar on the corner of Toll Road like?' It had looked okay from the outside when she'd walked past on the way to the bus that morning.

'Good basic food. Better music at the weekends.'

'We have a plan.' She stood up. 'I'd better be getting back. Can't have everyone thinking I'm a slacker.'

Lachlan laughed. 'As if.'

'I know, but I'm only a few days into the job and first impressions count.' Not that she'd made a mistake with anyone yet, and didn't intend to in the future, but it was best to tread carefully. One hang-up left over from the James days, she supposed, as she didn't used to be like this.

'Tilda, let it go. You are better than that.' Lachlan leaned back in his chair, watching her with an intensity that said he had her back.

She loved how he supported her, no questions asked, just like a real fiancé. 'You can be bossy when you choose.' Her smile was wide and genuine.

'Not that you take any notice,' he said with a laugh. 'Okay, see you later. I'll pick you up from home. We could walk to the pub but rain's forecast.'

'No surprise.' The clouds had been heavy when she'd come to work. There was a bounce in her step as she left the room, brought on by the ease with which she and Lachlan got on. It was as though they really *were* in a relationship. But they were in one of sorts. A fling maybe, but they'd still spent time together sharing the everyday things. She felt happier than she'd been in a long while. No way was she about to toss that away when it seemed as though she was finally getting her life in order the way she'd hoped.

'What do you think about taking the boys to Stanley Park next weekend, give Meredith time to have a coffee with the man she's seeing?' he asked.

'Sounds good. It wouldn't make for a good

date, dragging three boisterous boys along as well.'

'You two hit it off quickly on Sunday,' he said casually.

'I like Meredith. She's open and honest.'

'Always has been.'

She should be too. 'Are you as happy as everyone thinks?'

'Absolutely. You've touched me in ways I never thought would happen again.' His face became serious. 'We're good together. I only hope we're not racing blindly into something that might backfire on us both.'

She nodded. 'I try not to think like that. I mean, I came to stay with you while I looked for a place of my own, and have I done anything about that? No.' Was she meant to when she was supposedly his fiancée? Did she want to? It was all very well to think she might be falling for him, but reality mightn't work out the way she hoped. 'We've leapt into this with no discussion about what we actually want out of it.'

'It's not the normal way to start a relationship, for me, anyway, but I like what we're doing. Getting together and seeing how we go. We've clicked in so many aspects it feels good to just go with the flow.'

'I know what you're saying. But then I think

back to James and how wrong I was to believe he would never hurt me.' She'd never opened up much to Lachlan about her marriage. Right or wrong, it felt like the ideal time to now get some of this out there.

'Yes, and you left him when it got too much. That day he ranted at you for wrecking his car highlighted his true colours. He never stopped to ask how you were. He didn't talk to the surgeon or caregivers about your condition. He was only concerned for his car, for himself. You did the right thing, Tilda.'

'I don't doubt that for a moment. Never have. But sometimes I'm still shocked at how something he did or said can slam into my head. I can't help worrying that I might not be ready for a relationship yet, Lachlan.'

'You wouldn't be normal if you didn't think about the past,' he said with a smile. 'I think about Kelly and the agony of losing her. She was a big part of my life and is never going to go away completely. We both need to take our time with this. Neither of us wants to get hurt again. But meanwhile we can have a blast. Continue having amazing fun together, and get to know more about each other along the way.'

Just like that she relaxed again. Lachlan had a way of making her feel good about herself and her decisions. 'You're on.' They'd fallen into a fling, and now it seemed to be expanding into something more promising.

'He can't breathe!' a man shouted.

Tilda looked around and saw another man outside the elevator doors, clutching his throat while trying to gasp for air. She was at his side in seconds and pushing aside the first man, who was slapping his back. 'Stop that. Bend over,' she told the choking man. 'Now.'

The man's face was red and his eyes filled with fear.

'Thought you're supposed to hit them between the shoulder blades,' the other guy said.

Lachlan was there. 'He's got to bend over first or you could dislodge whatever's blocking his throat and make it drop further down his throat.'

Tilda pushed the man forward. 'Bend.' At last, he did.

Instantly she gave him a back blow, followed by four more.

Lachlan moved in beside her. 'I'll do the abdominal thrusts. He's a big man.'

And she was small against him. She got it. 'Go for it.' Grabbing the man's wrist, she felt his pulse. 'Weak. His lips are turning blue.'

As Lachlan gave the fifth abdominal thrust the man collapsed in his arms, and he staggered to hold him.

Tilda grabbed an arm to help lower the man to the floor. 'He's lost consciousness.'

'Someone call ED and ask them to send up an orderly with a bed,' Lachlan said as he straightened the man's body on the floor. Glancing at Tilda, he said, 'I'll start compressions.'

'I'll be ready to give him the breaths.'

Lachlan's nod was brief but there was satisfaction in his eyes. 'Good.'

At every thirtieth compression he sat back so she could give two long breaths into the man.

He did not react.

Sweat broke out on Lachlan's forehead. Compressions were no picnic. 'Thirty,' he called for the fifth time.

Leaning down, she breathed into the man again.

He hiccupped. Then coughed.

She grabbed his shoulders, rolled him onto his side as whatever had been blocking his throat finally came out. 'Phew.'

'I agree.' Lachlan was appraising the guy, reaching for his wrist to check his pulse.

'Has anyone got something clean to wipe his face with?' she asked over her shoulder. Taking the handful of paper tissues a woman passed her, she cleaned the man's face, keeping an eye on his chest to make sure he didn't stop breathing again.

'Pulse's good.'

'Lucky he was at a hospital,' the same woman said.

'He was very lucky,' Lachlan said to Tilda once the man had been taken to ED. 'You were onto the problem fast.'

'It still gives me a jolt when someone goes down like he did, but I do go straight into nurse mode.' It was instinctive, thank goodness.

'Confident and competent. Think I've said that before, mind.'

She blushed. Which was silly, but she couldn't stop the heat rising and expanding on her face. Compliments didn't come her way very often, and she especially liked those Lachlan gave her. 'Give over. You were equally competent and confident.'

'I'd better get back to Theatre or I won't be acting competently at all,' he said with a grin. 'See you later.'

CHAPTER EIGHT

A WEEK LATER, Lachlan did a double take and swallowed hard as he watched Tilda coming down the stairs in red heels that would've tripped him up on the first step.

The red dress she wore accentuated the amazing figure underneath, bringing thoughts of satin skin to his fingertips. He wanted to rush her back upstairs and tear it off her, to have her naked body under his again.

He took a step back. It wasn't happening. There wasn't time.

She swung a white jacket in one hand. Her hair hung loosely over the sides of her face, shining in the light. Her make-up was enough to accentuate her good features without looking like she'd plastered it on. Red lipstick highlighted those full lips, bringing more memories of exactly where those lips had performed their magic last night.

'You look stunning.'

'I haven't overdone it?'

He'd never seen her dressed like this. In Cambodia she'd been all about casual and comfortable. Nothing had changed since she'd returned home. It showed she had a few more surprises up her sleeve.

'Not at all. I don't want you to change a thing.'

She made it harder by the day to hold back from committing once and for all to her. As if he'd managed to hold back since the day he'd met her again. She'd sneaked in under his radar, become an essential part of his plan to grab a future for himself. A plan that increasingly included her at his side. He was falling for her, and it petrified him. It might be a very hard landing if she wasn't ready to commit. She'd been honest in telling him James had damaged her belief in herself. She was afraid of making the same mistake twice. He knew where she was coming from. He was deathly afraid of losing another person he loved.

For Tilda this was essentially a fling. No more, no less. It should be the same for him. Safer that way. Backing off and giving them both some space was the way to go, but it was impossible. Being with Tilda had brought him to life again and he was going to make the most of it. Who knew? His fears of being left alone again seemed to be subsiding but they weren't out of the picture yet. That would take more time, which he hoped he had.

'There again, we could go back upstairs and shuck all those clothes for another half an hour.'

She shook her head. 'I am not going to be the reason we're late for your parents' charity lunch.' Her laughter dried up and a frown appeared, but she said nothing.

'Don't be nervous. Everyone will be well behaved. Except maybe the boys. They love running around and making a racket, but they won't attack you. Normally they wouldn't be at one of these events but Dad figured they'd make things easier.' He grinned in an attempt to cheer her up. It must be daunting, given she knew no one apart from the boys and his parents and Meredith. And then there was the engagement factor. He might've made a big mistake accepting Tilda's idea for keeping his family at bay.

Tilda winced before lifting her head and locking a fierce look on him. 'I'll be fine.'

'I know you will.' He'd like nothing more than to carry her back upstairs and make love to her, but that was only delaying the inevitable. 'Dad always backs Mum with these charity occasions but he likes to have a bit of fun too. You're just an excuse to have the kids there.'

His father wrapped Tilda in a hug when they arrived. 'You look beautiful. No wonder Lachlan's fallen for you.'

Tilda blushed, but hugged him back. 'Stop it, John. You're embarrassing me.'

'Get on with making the most of what you two have started. It's right there in your faces and eyes whenever you look at each other. Everyone can see it.'

So much for thinking he could hide his true emotions. But he hadn't noticed Tilda being so transparent.

'You're just making it up.' Then he reached for Tilda's hand and got laughed at by his father. 'Come on. I'll show you round and introduce you to some people you might bump into at the hospital.' Anything to get away from his father right now.

Tilda squeezed his hand and made him feel needed. 'Let's get it over with.'

'It's not that bad.' Not really. They were having a fling with a bit more going on in their spare time. They made love every night. They shared not just his house, but his bedroom. They ate together at the end of the day and swapped stories about what they'd been doing at work. They were in a temporary relationship that might possibly expand into something more.

But she's worried she isn't ready for that.

She'd said so. She still didn't trust her own judgement and thought she might make the same mistake as she had with her ex.

But I would never, ever treat you like that, Tilda. You are your own woman.

'Hello, you two. You look lovely, Tilda. That dress is perfect on you.' His mother was beaming at them.

Right from one overenthusiastic parent to the other. Loving parent, he admonished himself. They cared so much about him, but couldn't they leave him to make his own decisions about what lay ahead?

'Hello, Faye.' Tilda sounded as though she suddenly wished she was anywhere else but here. Then she rallied. 'Is there anything I can do to help?'

'Not a thing. It's all organised and we get to relax and have some fun.'

'I'm looking forward to it.'

Lachlan doubted that. 'Let's grab a glass of champagne.' That'd help settle her nerves. He nodded at a passing waiter and handed Tilda a glass before taking one for himself. 'Come and meet my partners and their wives. They're all normal, nice folk and won't bite.'

She flicked him a small laugh. 'I'll be fine,' she ground through her teeth.

'Susie, Jason, I'd like you to meet Tilda.'

Tilda stepped up, shook hands all round and was soon talking to Susie about her time in Cambodia, and looking more relaxed by the minute.

'She fits in well with everyone,' Jason said.

Most of the time. 'She does.' He'd seen how easily she'd slid into the team in Phnom Penh, and from what he was hearing she was doing the same at Western G, but today was different, which could be because she'd never been to anything quite so extravagant. Hopefully that wouldn't put her off his family because these events were common amongst their friends. 'How's the house coming along?'

Jason and Susie were having a complete makeover done on their home and living in an apartment downtown while it was happening. Not something he could imagine doing. He and Kelly had loved the house when they'd bought it, though it did get a complete repaint job inside and out, along with new curtains, carpets and furniture. It still suited him. What if Tilda didn't like the décor? Was he prepared to change anything she didn't fancy? It would be a finish to all things Kelly. Not such a bad idea if he was starting out in a new relationship, though? Too many questions he wasn't quite ready to answer. Time to shut them down and get on with enjoying the luncheon party.

'Not fast enough, but when do building projects go to schedule?'

'When does anything?'

'When does anything what?' Tilda asked as she joined them.

'Go right when altering houses.'

'Not something I know anything about, I'm afraid.'

His mother appeared at Tilda's side and took her arm. 'Come on. There's someone I want to introduce you to. I think you'll find her delightful.'

Thirty minutes later Tilda returned, a woeful expression on her face. 'I've met the best dressmaker in town. An expert on wedding dresses apparently.'

Lachlan had to laugh. 'My mum can be OTT but she means well.'

'This is getting out of hand now,' Tilda sighed.

She was right, yet his heart felt heavy. If only they were a genuine couple, about to make plans for the future.

Back off, Lachlan. That's rushing things and you know you're not ready to do that either.

'I'll have words with Mum after this function is over, tell her you want to make your own decisions about anything we do.'

'Good. But go easy on her.'

Not everyone left at the end of the auction that raised thousands of dollars for the children's charity. Lachlan was tempted to hang around until the last two couples left but as they were his parents' closest friends he knew that could be hours away yet, so he took Tilda home and made coffee before discussing what to do.

'It's simple,' Tilda said. 'Tell your family we aren't getting married for a while and so there's no need to make wedding plans yet.' Then she sighed. 'Except weddings take a lot of planning, don't they? Couldn't we elope?' Her eyes widened. 'If we were really getting married, that is.'

Her words bit into him, slicing apart his tentative hope for more with her.

'Lachlan...'

Here it comes.

If not the decision to stop the fling before it got out of hand, then at least a request to slow down while they grappled with what they'd started.

A wobbly smile surprised him. 'I don't want to walk away from what we've got. We're only just getting going.'

A feather could have knocked him down. She was still with him, and wanted more. He should be running for the hills about now, but somehow he wasn't. Yet this was scary territory and he wondered if he was actually as ready as he'd hoped he was. It was as though her words were a warning not to forget how badly hurt he could be if something went wrong. How hurt both of them could get.

'But I can't deal with what your mother wants.'

'Fair enough. I would hate for you to regret being with me for however long we have.' He finally seemed to be moving on from his past to some extent. But he understood Tilda might need some space still. He could do that for her. It wouldn't be easy but it would be worth it in the end. And if it didn't work out? Then he'd move on; he would not go back to being that sad man he'd been before Tilda.

She came around the counter and snuggled into him, arms around his waist, breasts pressed into his chest. 'Thank you for understanding.' She tipped her head back and looked up at him. 'Or at least pretending you do.'

Bending down, he kissed her. Thoroughly. Which led to them going upstairs and making passionate love. For now, everything was right in his world.

* * *

The following afternoon the front door burst open and Campbell raced in, quickly followed by Lenny and Morgan. 'Lachlan, where are you? We're ready to go to the park with you.'

Lachlan fist pumped the air. 'So am I, guys. Tilda's coming too.' He still felt incredibly energised after an amazing night filled with truly great sex.

'Yippee,' shouted Morgan.

'Hi, you two.' Meredith appeared in the doorway, looking a little down.

'Meredith, it's good to see you,' Tilda said. Then she frowned in concern. 'Are you all right?'

'I cancelled my date.'

Tilda came across. 'Then you'd better come to the park with us instead.'

'Would you mind?'

'Wouldn't have said it if I did.' Tilda pulled out a stool at the counter. 'Take a pew. I've just made coffee. How do you have it?' She could say what she liked about not wanting to get too close too soon, but Lachlan could see Tilda had made herself at home in his house, as though she wanted to stay.

'Black with one.'

The boys were looking impatient. 'Thought

we were going to Stanley Park *now*,' Lenny whined.

'I'm not quite ready,' Lachlan told them. 'How about you go to the shed and get my bag with the soccer balls and rugby ball in it?'

'All right...' Lenny dragged out the words as if it was such a big deal to do what they'd been asked.

'You get cold feet with your date?' Tilda was asking Meredith.

'Sort of. He's almost too enthusiastic, if you know what I mean. Keeps saying we should spend the whole weekend together. He says the boys are included in that, but I don't want to rush them into something that might not work out. They could get hurt if they expect too much, too soon.'

'It seems like you're walking a fine line between following your own needs and looking out for them. Err on the side of caution, maybe?'

Just like she was doing, Lachlan knew. She had said as much, but hearing her now really brought it home to him. Should he be doing the same? The potential to be hurt himself was loud and clear. But they got on so well, and when they made love he felt so close to her it was as though they were one person. They were like that in more ways than one too.

He stood up. 'I'll see how the boys are getting on finding the ball bag.'

'You all right with me joining you?' Meredith asked him with a worried look.

'Of course I am.'

'Why can't I chase them?' Four-year-old Morgan stood an hour later, hands on hips, mimicking Lachlan as he stared down the Canadian geese.

'Because you'll frighten them. If you haven't already with all the noise you're making.'

'They're too big to be scared,' Morgan shouted. He only had one volume when he was talking.

'Come on, let's kick a few balls. Not at the geese either,' he added quickly as a gleam entered Campbell's eyes.

'First one to kick a ball between those two trees is a winner,' Tilda called as she bounced a soccer ball with one hand. 'I'm going to beat you all.' She tipped an assortment of balls onto the ground.

Bedlam ensued.

'I want that one!'

'Can't. It's mine!'

'I'm having it.'

'Boys, no arguing. One each. It doesn't matter which ball you have, I've got the winning one,' Tilda teased, which got the result she intended.

Lenny kicked his tennis ball hard and it bounced in the opposite direction to the trees Tilda had pointed to. He grabbed another ball for a second attempt.

'I'll be the goalkeeper,' Meredith announced. 'I couldn't kick a paper bag to save myself.'

'Watch out, Morgan. Line the ball up so you are looking straight at the trees. That's it.' Tilda knelt down and held the ball lightly. 'Now, kick it hard. That's it. Way to go.'

The ball dribbled about ten metres.

Lachlan pretended to kick another ball and made sure it went in the wrong direction, all the while listening to Tilda laughing and talking Lenny through another kick. She was doing something so simple and yet she was clearly happy. She was making the boys happy too. His chest filled with warmth. She mightn't have had siblings or been surrounded with other kids but she instinctively seemed to know what they needed. Attention and fun.

Did she think about having children? She'd be a great mother. There was a big heart in that beautiful chest, if only she could free it up and start living the life she must've hoped for with her horrendous ex. He remembered that day in Cambodia when Bebe was having surgery and the look of wonder on Tilda's face when she'd picked her up. She'd touched her abdomen and made him wonder if she might've been pregnant some time. Now he knew she had been, and it had ended tragically. She had to be wary of trying again.

'Lachlan, look out!' she yelled.

Instinctively he ducked and a soccer ball flew past his head. He spun around to find Campbell laughing at him. 'You little rotter. I'll show you where to kick the ball.' He retrieved the ball and lined it up with the trees. Fingers crossed it went somewhere near the makeshift goal. Sometimes it paid to get one in, right in front of the kids.

When the boys started tiring, long after Lachlan was ready to give up chasing balls and boys, everyone clambered into the large four-wheel drive and they headed to a take-out for burgers and chips.

'A perfect end to a great afternoon,' Tilda said before biting into her chicken burger.

'I'll say.' It had been fun and, best of all, he was pleased she'd enjoyed herself getting to know the kids. It said a lot to him about her. Another plus. There were getting to be a lot of those. He had finally started to open up his heart again and this was the reward. If only Tilda could see how amazing it could be for them both. In the meantime, he'd try and remain careful. Probably too late for his heart to remain completely unscathed, but hopefully he'd still survive if it all went belly-up.

Then she smiled across the table at him. A big, happy smile just for him. 'I haven't had so much fun since we were in Cambodia.'

Lachlan dropped the negative thoughts. Trying to second-guess all the things that could go wrong was exhausting and only wasted the good times spent with Tilda. 'Here's to more fun times where they came from.'

She nodded. 'I agree.'

'I'm going to look at an apartment on Twelfth after work, so I'll be late home,' Tilda told Lachlan when she saw him coming out of Theatre three weeks later.

'You'll do anything to get out of cooking, won't you?' He might be joking but she could sense that sadness lay behind his words and it gave her hope.

'I'll get pizza on the way home.' She didn't really want to find a place to buy, but ultimately her plan hadn't changed. She had money to invest in a property and, while she was living with Lachlan there was no hurry to purchase something, she'd decided to start looking in case the day came when she had to move out of his home in a hurry. She was only doing what she had to, to protect herself in case things went wrong.

Being engaged to Lachlan should be the best time of her life, but it wasn't real. The negative side of her brain kept preparing for the day when they decided to call quits on the engagement. Though she was giving their fling everything she had, she was worried it wasn't going to last. Lachlan seemed happy enough right now, but there'd been no indication he wanted more than what they had. His family had accepted her place in his life, but soon they'd start asking when the wedding would happen—if it was ever going to. They were supposed to be just *going with the flow*, after all. Having *fun times*. And even though she'd agreed to that, suddenly she wanted much more, and she was deathly afraid he didn't.

'I'd better go. The next patient is in the pre-op waiting room and I just saw Mrs Jackson heading into the scrub room.' That at least was real.

'Tilda…' Lachlan paused, drew a breath. 'How about I come with you to look at the place, and then we go somewhere for a meal afterwards?'

'You don't mind looking at an apartment

with me?' It didn't really fit the picture of them together, enjoying a hot, heavy fling.

His shrug was nonchalant, and covering up something. Moving towards the day when they split up? 'If we get to have a decent meal afterwards I'm happy.'

'I'll wait for you after work. My appointment with the agent is for six o'clock. Will you be able to make it?'

'I'm not operating this afternoon, and my last patient is due in the office at five. Meet you at the car.' He turned and headed away before she could answer.

Not that she had anything more to say, other than to ask where this was going. The idea of looking at apartments for herself, let alone signing up for one, made her feel sick. When she'd left Cambodia she'd been looking forward to getting on with her life back here. That had included finding somewhere nice to live, a place with more space than she'd had in the past because she'd be there long-term. Now the idea of living on her own wasn't cheering her up one tiny bit, but she owed it to herself to at least have a backup plan in place. Falling for Lachlan and having no idea how he felt about her had made her feel incredibly vulnerable. She had to do this.

'Matilda? Are you all right?' Allie called. 'We're ready to go in here.'

Allie, another nurse, was fast becoming a friend at work. Shaking away the gloom in her head, Tilda forced a smile on her face and headed to the scrub room. 'I'm all good.' Then she yawned, feeling sluggish at the same time.

'A late night?'

'Quite the opposite.' She and Lachlan had been curled up in bed by ten, which was early for them. For the first time since she'd returned from Cambodia they hadn't made love, as she'd fallen asleep within minutes of pulling the sheet up to her chin. So why this tiredness? 'Could be the busy weekend catching up with me.' Most likely it was due to the stress of living with Lachlan and loving him while feeling incredibly insecure about where they were headed and frightened she was making a mistake. Throw in unexpected hours yesterday, with two unscheduled operations resulting from a car accident and a man falling off scaffolding at a building site, and she'd all but crawled home afterwards.

Not home, Tilda. It's Lachlan's house.

She was there temporarily.

I don't want to move out. I want to stay. With Lachlan.

But that might not be on the cards. Deep

breath. She needed to relax. She was going to see an apartment tonight that, from what was on the website, ticked all the boxes on her need-to-have list. She could ring up now and say she'd take it. But she wouldn't. She didn't step blindly into anything. Especially not love.

'What do you think?' the agent asked Tilda. 'I have to tell you I have two more people booked to view this property tomorrow.'

'It's cosy,' she answered, rubbing her hands up and down her arms. It would be if the heating was on.

'Not too small?' Lachlan asked. He looked a little stunned as he gazed around the top-level apartment, ducking to avoid banging his head on the slanting roof.

Matilda winked. 'It's built for shorties like me.'

'Places like this are in high demand,' the agent advised.

Then how come it was still available after being advertised for two weeks? 'It's a handy location for my work and going to the beach.' Buses ran along Burrard, which was close by, so there was no problem getting to work and back. She returned to the bedroom for another look.

'By the time you put a bed in here there

won't be any room for anything else.' Lachlan was right behind her.

Nothing new for her. 'Unless I decide to live further out of town, this is the reality of what I can afford.' He'd probably be thinking his wardrobe was bigger than this room. 'Besides, I don't have a lot of furniture. Just shoes,' she added with a little laugh. Shoes were her new hobby. Two pairs in ten days. Not bad for her. Seeing the look of wonder on Lachlan's face when she'd walked down the stairs on the day they were going to his parents' charity event had made her feel sexy and attractive. All because of a pair of shoes. Maybe the tight red dress with the slightly revealing top had had something to do with it too.

'Seen enough?' He made it sound as though there hadn't been much to see in the first place. But then he did live in a mansion.

'I have.' In the lounge she told the agent, 'I'll think about it and get back to you.'

'You might miss out if you don't make an instant decision.'

'I'll take that chance.' This was the first place she'd looked at so far. The problem being that not many seemed to be available in the areas she'd prefer at a price that didn't bankrupt her. But looking around at the small, tidy space she just didn't feel the vibe. It didn't give her that sense of home. Getting picky? Spoilt after staying with Lachlan? Or not ready to move away from him? 'Thank you for showing me the apartment,' she said brusquely and headed downstairs and out of the front door.

'Where to next?' Lachlan asked once they were settled in his car.

'There's a unit on Burrard I'd like to drive by.'

'It's dark.'

'Just do it, okay?'

He started the car and pulled out. 'Burrard's a main road. It'll be too noisy for you.'

Exactly why the road wasn't her desired location, but she couldn't afford to be too fussy if she wanted to be this close to the city centre.

'I can wear earmuffs,' she snapped. He had no idea how the other half lived.

'Hey.' Lachlan laid his hand on her knee. 'I got a shock seeing that place. It was clean and tidy, but so small. Even for a shortie.' His smile was tired. 'I know I haven't got a clue what you can afford or what's available, but it really took me aback to see that.'

'Can't fault your honesty.' Her heart squeezed. He was always honest with her. She loved that about him. Most of the time. 'I've been saving hard but I can't afford what I really want, so I'm going for the next best thing, just to get on the property ladder.'

The money she had in her investment account wasn't quite enough for the kind of property she longed for. A small house with a little lawn so she could have a garden and a swing for her child, should she ever have that baby she yearned for. Her mind filled with the picture of Lachlan's huge lawns. She could have more than one child there. Problem with that was she wasn't set up for one child, let alone multiple children. They didn't need wealth or two parents, but she'd have to work full-time to support a child and she knew what it was like to come home to an empty house after school. Grandma had worked long hours to provide her with the basics, and she'd do the same, but those empty hours with a distracted babysitter waiting for her to come home were a constant reminder of what she needed to consider carefully.

'What number Burrard?'

Tapping her phone, the address she'd put in earlier came up on the finder app. 'There you go.'

Within minutes they were pulling up outside a property overgrown with knee-deep grass and weeds. Three old cars were parked at angles on the drive and lawn. The house was in darkness.

'This can't be it.' Lachlan was peering through the windscreen, a frown marring his looks.

Looking from the photo on her phone to the house and back, she swallowed the bile that had risen in her throat. 'They spruced up the photo for sure. The unit is supposedly around the back. Who knows? It might be in better condition, but I wouldn't want to be living behind this.'

Pulling back out onto the road, Lachlan said quietly, 'Like I said, there's no hurry to move out of my place. You've only seen two properties so far. Take your time and get it right.'

Again she swallowed. This time it was tears that needed getting rid of. The problem with his suggestion was that she was more than comfortable in his house and the longer it took to find her own place the harder it would be to go. 'The thing is, despite the last few weeks, I don't really know where we're at, Lachlan.'

Lachlan braked, pulled over and parked. Turning to face her, he said, 'What do *you* want, Tilda? Do you want to move out?'

'It wouldn't mean we won't see each other any more if I did. Would it?' It wouldn't be the same though, if she moved into her own place.

They'd have to make plans to see each other, not bump into one another beside the bench or under the shower. Did she want that? Not really, but neither did she want to keep living this way. She needed to sort herself out once and for all. 'I don't know how long I can keep up the pretence that we're engaged.'

'I thought you were happy.'

'So did I. Yet suddenly I'm doubting everything.' It could be a passing fear, the past tripping her up. She hoped so. But she suspected it was more to do with her unrequited feelings.

Lachlan nodded. 'Fair enough. We did start out in a rush. But then flings are like that.'

So it was still a fling for him, nothing more serious. Her heart sank. 'What if we went on some dates? Like we were getting to know each other?'

He flinched. 'You don't think we're already doing that?'

Kind of. 'I'd like time to get used to being in a relationship after striving so hard to sort my life out and get back on my feet.' Reaching for his hand, she gripped it, putting aside some of her doubts. 'Are we in a relationship?' Because she could admit that she wanted to be, even if the thought scared her.

'I am.'

Her heart expanded, opened a little more.

'I'm with you. Just not quite as we've been doing it so far.'

Lifting their joined hands, he kissed hers. 'Here's to us and seeing where we're headed then.'

Relief filled her. Leaning over, she found his mouth with hers and kissed with all her need. She mightn't be certain where they were going but she knew she wanted to find out. If she gave him more time, perhaps he would fall in love with her too?

They never did get to eat pizza. Toast in bed after making out between the sheets was the best they managed.

Lachlan couldn't get that apartment out of his head. It was ridiculously small. How could Matilda even contemplate living in such a cramped space? She was probably used to it, whereas not in a million years could he see himself in something the size of a matchbox. His house was too large for one person, but he hadn't been able to bring himself to sell it when Kelly died.

These days the walls didn't resonate with her laughter. He didn't hear her talking to him, didn't even pause to listen for her. Like her scent on the pillows, the sounds had faded away.

I have moved on.

He was more than ready to start living life to the full again.

Just like that, his gaze lifted to Tilda, curled up beside him under the sheet. Even in sleep she looked shattered. And beautiful. Yeah, but the real reason behind his dislike of the apartment was that Tilda was apparently contemplating moving out of here, into her own place, when he'd thought they were getting on so well.

Sliding down the bed, he tucked her in against his body, holding her like he'd never let her go. Because he didn't want to. But he had to. She wanted a place to call her own. If he didn't accept that she'd probably cut him out of her life completely.

Life without Tilda looked impossible from where he lay. So he'd have to make sure they kept getting on as well as this and hopefully she'd finally stop looking for a home of her own and agree to live here, with him.

Home. At the moment this was his, but he'd like to make it theirs. His breath stalled in his lungs. He'd fallen for her more deeply than he'd known. Tilda was beautiful inside and out. She was everything he wanted for the future—his wife, the mother for his children, the woman he'd come home to every night or be there for her when she arrived back from a day at work.

But did she want the same thing after everything she'd been through? He wasn't sure.

And if something went horribly wrong with their relationship, would he ever get back on his feet again? He doubted he could. It had been hard enough when he'd lost Kelly, and then Matt. A shudder rocked him. And here he'd been thinking he'd moved on. Conquered his fears. Maybe not so much after all.

Under his arm, Tilda rolled over, her eyes still closed. Then her hand covered his crotch.

'Damn you to the end of the bed and back, Tilda Simmons. I have to have you.'

She was all over him in an instant, her mouth on his neck, her tongue making hot sweeps on his skin and sending shafts of desire scorching down his body to where it all came to a blinding head.

'Tilda,' he groaned as he lifted her head and covered her mouth with his hungry one. His tongue plunged into her, tasting, searching, feeling her heat, her need throbbing through her.

Her hands were on his butt, kneading and caressing in incredibly sexy moves, making him harder than rock. So hard he was going to explode if he didn't have her right then. *Deep breath. Hold on. Not so fast.* His fingers found her heat, her moist spot, slid over her.

She rocked against him, cried, 'Lachlan…'

'Wait,' he said aloud as he reached for a condom. Then he touched her again, his fingers moving back and forth, back and forth, making her hotter and wetter, and turning himself into a molten heap of need and want at the same time.

'Now,' she begged. 'Now, Lachlan. Please.'

He couldn't deny her. He plunged into her heat, deeper and deeper, again and again, until she cried against him. Within moments he was following her into a place that had no boundaries or fears or questions, only wonder and amazement and a bone-deep satisfaction.

CHAPTER NINE

SATURDAY MORNING TWO weeks later and they
had the weekend all to themselves. Lachlan
had no plans at all, other than maybe to take
Tilda out to collect some of her gear from her
lock-up. Something she'd been going to do ever
since she'd arrived home but hadn't quite got
around to, other than to get a bag of clothes
early on.

'I feel terrible.' Tilda suddenly shoved her
plate of toast away and leapt up to run out of
the room.

She did look pasty, but they hadn't had a
lot of sleep last night, being busy between the
sheets, so to speak. He followed her through
to the bathroom, getting there as the door
slammed behind her.

'Hey, what's up?'

Then he heard a retching sound and shoved
open the door. 'I'm coming in.'

She was sitting back on her haunches, holding her hair away from her face, looking rattled. 'Did I eat something off?'

'We had steak and salad last night. I can't see that giving you food poisoning.' But she had been more tired than usual lately. Sometimes she'd even been quite pale.

Oh, no.

'Tilda? When was your last period?'

She stared at him, her mouth an O shape. 'Not that.' She shook her head. 'It can't be that. We've been so careful.'

They had. 'Every time.' Passing her a cloth to wipe her face, he knelt down beside her. 'Condoms aren't one hundred percent guaranteed to do their job.' He'd seen the result of that often enough as a trainee doctor.

'I should've gone on the pill.'

Hindsight was a wonderful thing.

'We're probably wrong, but to be on the safe side we'd better find out for certain.'

She closed her eyes and her hands gripped the cloth as she scrubbed her face and mouth. Then she swore. Opening tired eyes, she stared at him. 'Seriously? Someone—something's having a joke on us. Trying to make this fake engagement real.'

He shot to his feet. 'No way.' This had nothing to do with that. It would not be the catalyst to making their fake engagement real. That would only happen if they both wanted it.

'I might not be pregnant.'

'I think you are. Unfortunately.' His teeth were grinding. Becoming a father should have been a decision for him and Tilda to make, not some random occurrence. But he should know better than most how life threw those out there whenever it chose. This was why he'd been so adamant he was remaining single. Until Tilda came along and rocked him to his core. So much for taking their time while they worked out where they were headed.

Shock replaced Tilda's bewilderment. 'Lachlan, slow down. You're overreacting before we've even found out for certain I'm pregnant. Sure, get a kit and then we will know one way or the other and can make some decisions based on fact.'

He reached down and helped her to her feet gently, remorse for his reaction nudging the shock to one side. 'We can work through this. We *will* work through it.' He wanted to say *together*, but he wasn't certain how she'd react to that. Tilda didn't really do impulsive—other than when they were in bed. She'd want time to figure out how she felt about them together and now there was no time.

'Go. Get the test kit so we know where we

stand. I need to know for certain.' She turned away, but not before he saw the despair filling her eyes.

He had the feeling she was referring to their relationship more than the possibility of a baby. Their relationship that was loving and caring and had meant so much more to him than it was ever supposed to. Damn it. Of course he'd support Tilda. The baby was theirs, not hers. He was its father. If there was a baby.

'Tilda, I *am* here for you. All the way.' Again, that mental picture of her with that little girl, Bebe, back in Phnom Penh, and the longing on her face loomed up in his mind. If she was pregnant she'd go through with it. He had no doubt whatsoever. She would love and cherish their baby for ever. As he would. All his previous fears slammed back into his head, waking him up to reality—falling for Tilda had made him vulnerable again. But so was she. And he would be there for her all the way. 'Tilda…'

She spun around and snapped, 'Just go and get the kit.'

A longing to hold her until the raw pain left her face, to tell her how he felt about her, filled him. He took a step towards the woman who'd changed his life and helped him get back on track when he'd believed he'd lost direction for ever. But all he could say was, 'We'll make it work. It will be all right.'

'Sure, Lachlan. Is this when you remind me you didn't want a relationship ever again? Don't want children because you might love them and then lose them?' Agony etched her face. 'I'm not staying around to listen to your answers. I'll pack my bag while you go get that blasted kit.'

His heart split open. All over again. He'd probably just gone and blown any chance he might've had with Tilda. He should have known that it was already way too late for his heart to ever recover from losing her. He loved her to the moon and back. But if he told her that now would she believe him, or would she think he was just trying to claim his baby? Losing her was the one thing he'd hoped to avoid by not getting involved. But there were more ways of losing someone than from a runaway car or a heart attack.

So fix it. Be different this time.

His heart quailed at the thought of stepping off that cliff. It would mean burying his fears for ever. Could he even do that? He had to be sure.

'No, Tilda, I will never leave you to deal with this alone. You matter to me. If you are pregnant our baby will also matter to me.'

She stared at him.

He wanted to admit his love, but at the last second he choked. 'Don't go, Tilda,' was all he could say in that moment.

Don't go, Tilda.

'Meaning? Stay for an hour? A day? For ever?' she asked through the despair knocking at her heart. She so wanted a baby but she wasn't ready in every way conceivable. Bad choice of word, that.

Lachlan wasn't heading out yet. 'I don't know what will happen if we find out for sure we're having a baby, but I can't live with the thought of you walking out of here with nowhere to go. Nowhere that you'll be comfortable staying anyway.'

The intensity in his expression made her pause the whirling thoughts in her mind. 'You're concerned about where I might go? That's it?'

'No, that came out all wrong. We are in this together, regardless of where our relationship is at. You must stay here, at least until we have talked about things.'

Must? Telling her what to do? Sounded familiar to her. Her heart broke into pieces. 'You think?'

'In the end, the choice about where you stay

is up to you, but for now can we at least get an answer and then talk about it?'

'Fair enough.' She had been about to run off without talking through the consequences of being pregnant. She didn't know for certain she was yet. Oh, yes, she did. Her hand stroked her belly. It might be churning like a washing machine through nerves and fear of losing everything again, but she was pregnant. She felt it in her heart. She'd known this sense of protectiveness last time. Last time she'd miscarried. That couldn't happen again.

'I'll shift into one of the spare bedrooms.' Until she found an apartment. The first one that was available for rent would do; she didn't have to wait to buy one. But she wasn't being fair to Lachlan. He was in this as much as she was. He hadn't said he wanted nothing to do with the baby. In fact he'd been adamant he'd be there for them. Not a familiar reaction from a man she cared about, then. But enough to make major decisions about her future? Her child's future?

His mouth softened a fraction. 'Thank you.'

What about them? There was a lot to talk about and now the pregnancy could influence their decisions in ways that might not be so good for their relationship. She knew she loved him, but he'd never even hinted that he loved her too. But first things first. They needed certainty about the baby.

'I'll still be here when you get back, Lachlan, I promise.'

'Thanks.'

She watched him go, his steps the heaviest she'd ever known as he crossed the hall to the internal door into the garage. Her heart sank lower and lower by the minute, which had nothing to do with the baby. She loved Lachlan with all her heart. It had taken this to wake her up to what that really meant. Because she already knew, despite his optimism, he wasn't ready for a permanent relationship. He seemed to have changed over the past weeks, accepting her into his life in every way possible, even when she'd had her own doubts. Now reality had slammed into him hard and she suspected marriage wasn't on the cards for them. That would mean putting Kelly aside for ever and he might never be ready to do that. Just as she'd struggled to let go of how James had taken over and controlled every aspect of her life. She doubted Lachlan would ever be like James, but it had been so hard to trust her judgement enough to let the past go.

Lachlan looked like she felt—stunned and confused. Fair enough. She got it. But there'd also been a look of withdrawal on his face, despite saying he'd be there for her. For them. Could she love enough for both of them? Did she want to try? Not really. She loved Lachlan but he had to come to her with his heart in his hands or it wasn't ever going to work. She knew that from painful experience.

And until he was ready for that, whatever they'd had between them was over. Even if the test was negative, she wouldn't be getting back into bed with Lachlan. Nor chatting over a meal about anything and everything, or working together to help others less fortunate. This had been a wake-up call for them both. They'd got on so well, had the same dreams and hopes, but now she realised they both had to work out what they really wanted, emotionally and romantically, to be able to meet each other halfway.

She sank against the basin and dropped her face into shaking hands. What a mess. There was nothing fake about the love for Lachlan filling her heart. Nothing. From the moment the thought she was pregnant struck, her first instinct had been to reach out to him—because she loved him so, so much. Yet while he'd said he'd be there for them, he hadn't sounded like the affectionate, caring man she'd come to know over the past weeks.

Which only went to show she'd gone and

done what she'd sworn never to do again—fallen in love with a man who wasn't able to share his heart. Lachlan was everything she wanted and that meant he wasn't a control freak. But he had his own baggage and he still wasn't letting her in, wasn't about to discuss his issues properly and see if they could make it work between them. What would he do if she miscarried? Support her for a while and then disappear out of her life?

Naturally he wanted to protect his heart. Like she did hers, only it was too late for her. But whatever Lachlan felt for her, he wouldn't be admitting it. That would be too risky for him.

So she'd have to get busy and find an apartment, fast. She needed her own space. Avoiding Lachlan in his home would only add to the nightmare.

Straightening up, she studied her face in the mirror. Awful didn't begin to describe her blotchy cheeks and sad eyes. Sad? When she was having a baby? The baby she'd longed for ever since the day she'd lost her first one. Even when she wasn't prepared, financially or otherwise, she couldn't wait to carry this baby through to full term and beyond. She would not lose it this time. Lachlan would love his child too, however he felt about her. He had a big heart, loved his family and friends.

So she'd carry on as though everything would work out and the baby would arrive safely in a few more months, happy and healthy.

Put the baby first in everything you do from now on.

Was she up to that? Absolutely. She loved it already. No argument. This was where tough got tougher. She was strong. She now had to be even stronger for her baby's sake. The baby she refused to miscarry.

The doorbell pealed loud in the empty house. Who was that? Lachlan's parents and Meredith and her tribe always bowled in, didn't stop for a closed door, so it couldn't be any of them. Fingers crossed. She wasn't up to facing them at the moment. Her feet dragged as she made her way to the front door. The bell rang again.

'Coming,' she growled, then pulled the door open.

A courier stood there, holding out a letter pack. 'This is for Matilda Simmons.'

'That's me. Do you need proof?'

'No. Only a signature.'

A quick scrawl and she was back inside, closing the door as she stared at the envelope. A sticker with the law office logo was on the back. The divorce papers had finally arrived.

'Great timing.' Biting down on her frustration, she went to get some scissors and opened the pack to tip out the paperwork.

As she stared at the legal proof signifying the end of her marriage, tears began sliding down her cheeks. So many failed dreams culminating in a single piece of paper. It wasn't that she missed her ex, or even cared where he was or what he was up to. It was how her hopes and wishes had all come down to this. Would her time with Lachlan end in a similar fashion? Not divorce but over just the same. *Finito.*

'Tilda? What's happened now? What's that paper?' Lachlan was back.

She knew he wouldn't have dallied on the way.

'Tilda?' Worry spilled out of him.

'I'm officially divorced.' Her lawyer had said as much in his email yesterday, but seeing the signed paper brought a large dose of reality. It was what she'd wanted, but it still caused her to ache inside, knowing she'd been so wrong about a man she'd once been devoted to.

'You're free again.' He was tense, and he spoke sharply.

She fought the need to reach out to him for a hug and stepped away. 'I am.'

Not if I'm pregnant, because a baby is a life-long commitment.

One she wasn't quite ready for, but would do all in her power to prepare for regardless.

'You got the testing kit?'

'Yes.' He handed over a small package.

Her fingers were shaking as she took it. 'Crunch time.' And she didn't mean positive or negative. Whatever the result, their relationship was over, but it was going to get awkward sharing this place, even if only for a few days.

At the bathroom door she turned around to look at Lachlan. He was watching her, his face so sad she had to fight not to rush over and throw her arms around him and promise they could make everything all right. He'd resist and she couldn't face that. He had to want to be a father, to want to be with her. Want her, and love her, not just offer to support her out of kindness or duty. She shuddered. No, thank you. She would manage on her own, no matter what was thrown at her.

'I'll be right here,' he said as he sank onto a stool by the counter.

Supporting her? Or desperate to know the result? Probably both. Lachlan wouldn't desert her at this moment.

'Then let's get this done,' she muttered as she closed the door and tore open the packet. Introspection was only delaying finding out one way or the other what lay ahead. Not that she didn't already know.

A few minutes later she laid the result in front of Lachlan. 'I'm pregnant.' Her heart was pounding, making her throat feel blocked and her head spin.

He stared at the blue line for so long she wondered if he'd fallen asleep. Except that was impossible, given the state he was in.

'You're not saying much,' she jibed as all her emotions gelled into shock.

'I'm afraid to utter a word.'

'Lachlan, this is me, Matilda. I have never deliberately done a thing to upset you, so why not discuss this with me?'

'It's not what you might say that worries me.' He finally turned in his chair to look at her. 'I've screwed up big time.'

She was aghast at the pain and despair in his face. 'I've been a part of everything that's happened too.'

'I tried to stay away from you, Tilda. But you got to me so easily.' He shook his head, despair darkening his beautiful face. 'When you came to Vancouver it was impossible not to get closer to you after our time in Cambodia. You're so beautiful and sexy and you steal my breath away every time I look at you.'

This sounded good. She should be feeling happy and ready for something good to come. But this was Lachlan. He was about to pour cold water on his words. It was there in the way he drew himself up and locked those formidable blue eyes on her. She waited, her heart still pounding so loud it was a wonder she could hear herself think.

'Nothing's changed, Matilda. I'm still afraid of losing someone. But I'll always be here, supporting you, doing what's right.'

Back to calling her Matilda. He couldn't have worded it any clearer. Suddenly she was angry. She didn't want the right thing done by her. She wanted his love or nothing.

'Can't? Or won't? Whatever you think, this is real, and it's not going away. I am pregnant with *our* baby. Get used to the idea.'

He rose out of his chair to lean against the counter. 'I am well aware *we* are having a child. It scares the hell out of me.'

'You think I'm not worried too?' She should be grateful he was being honest, but it would be good to have him with her in everything that lay ahead. Their baby needed its father to be there for it and to love it unconditionally. Not to have him pull down the blinds the moment he learned the baby really existed. 'Has it occurred to you that I'm already afraid of losing it?'

'Oh, Matilda, please don't think that. Baby will be fine. Strong like its mum.'

'Her father's strong too. But I've already lost one.' Her? Yes, she was having a girl. She knew it like she'd known she was pregnant. It was in her genes to have a daughter. 'To lose this one would decimate me.'

He looked at her. 'I know.'

He probably did. 'Talk to me, tell what you're feeling right now.'

Get the problem out in the open so we can deal with it.

'I never believed we'd be facing this dilemma. I just want you to be happy.' He paused, watching her the whole time. 'You can always live here. Permanently,' he added in a rush. 'Or at least until we've had time to really consider all the options and think about our baby's future.' He wasn't saying anything about his feelings for her, which said a lot more than he realised.

It had only been a fling after all. He hadn't stopped fearing the worst would happen again.

'So I can live here as a flatmate and the mother of your child? No thanks.' Impossible when she loved him so much.

She felt her grandmother's hand on her

shoulder, as she often had when she was growing up, telling her she was strong and capable of standing alone and raising her child to become strong too. Lachlan would have a part in the child's life but not hers. She was not waiting around for him to reject her. Her heart wasn't so strong it wouldn't break. She did believe she could trust him not to try and control her, but he'd never love her the way he'd loved Kelly. She couldn't live with that.

'You have to do what's best for you, Lachlan. But please don't waste a wonderful opportunity to have the life you might really want.'

With that, she turned and strode away, head high and heart slamming. Her hands were fists at her sides. Her stomach was one large knot of frustration and anger and sorrow. That man held her heart in his hands and didn't know it. She'd started to believe she was ready to chance everything again, to love and be loved. The reality was she was single, and going to stay that way. But there was a baby growing inside her so she'd have to calm down and work at being relaxed, so as not to send sour vibes throughout her body and upset her baby. Her daughter had to stay safe. Her heart didn't matter half as much.

Liar.

* * *

Lachlan watched Matilda storm upstairs. His heart went with her.

I love her.

Without a doubt. That didn't stop the fear of losing her ramping up to full speed. Or of something terrible happening to their baby. It was terrifying. First Kelly, then Matt. If that happened again to Tilda or their baby— Then he'd be lost for ever, even worse off than before. Except he already stood to lose her because of the way he felt about her.

If he told her the truth, he might have Tilda at his side as they went through life, loving each other and their child. Children plural. As if. He couldn't deal with the knowledge of one baby on the way, let alone multiple. Face it, he wasn't dealing with anything very well right now.

Go talk to her.

And say what? He wanted to protect her, make her life easy so that she wasn't at risk of miscarrying again because of added stress. She'd already lost one baby; she'd suffer badly if she lost this one too. So he had to look out for her. That was who he was, unless it came to protecting his heart. He'd stuffed up there. He'd already given that to her. And she didn't know it. Nor did she probably want to know now. He'd started retreating emotionally from her the moment it dawned on him she might be pregnant. The commitment and involvement of being a father wasn't the problem. It was the overwhelming love he'd have for her and his child and the fear of losing them that was causing the pain in his heart and the tension in his gut.

You love Tilda. You'll love the baby the moment you accept it.

That was what got to him. He would love his child from here to the end of the earth and back again if he let it in. As he already did his baby's mother. She'd got under his skin, into his head and heart, and there was no coming back from that. But she didn't want him or his love, did she? She had her baby to love, and he would help her raise it as he'd promised.

His phone vibrated on the bench. Snatching it up, he snapped, 'Yes?'

'Lachlan, I'm Anna, a nurse on the surgical ward. Sorry to bother you on your weekend off, but Millie Jackson's complaining of severe pain at the surgical site. The plastic surgeon on call is in Theatre and I don't think we can wait.'

'I'll come in.' He shoved the phone into his pocket, snatched up the keys to his four-wheel drive and headed for the door. Something else to think about, however briefly, might be good for his messed-up brain. Except he couldn't just walk out on Tilda without saying a word.

Upstairs, he found her in his bedroom collecting her clothes into a pile. No doubt moving into another room. 'I've been called in to see a patient I operated on yesterday.'

'Fine.'

No, it wasn't. But what could he say? At the moment anything that came out of his mouth wouldn't have been thought through enough. He had no clear idea of what he wanted to offer Tilda, other than his love and support, and neither of those was enough, considering how badly he'd already hurt her.

'See you later.'

Her reply was a shrug, as though she'd already moved on from him. And why wouldn't she? He wasn't making anything easier for her. Which wasn't how this was meant to be.

The drive in to the hospital was tedious. He'd done it so often he could probably do it blindfolded. It certainly wasn't distracting his busy mind. Nor did his patient. The pain in her abdomen where he'd done a minor tummy tuck was high, but the reason was not apparent. Until she admitted to bending over sharply to snatch up a mascara brush she'd dropped over the side of the bed. An X-ray showed a minor bleed that had stopped quickly.

'No more bending unless you want to return to Theatre for more surgery,' he said firmly. Too firmly by the look on the nurse's face. But he wasn't having a great day.

Heading out of the hospital, he made a snap decision and grabbed the walking shoes from his vehicle. Going home wasn't an option. It would be too uncomfortable, worrying about bumping into Tilda all the time.

Tilda or Matilda. There was a huge gap between the two versions of her name. One was professional and friendly without being close. The other was his woman, soft and fun and loving. And he'd let her go because he was afraid of losing her. His heart dropped to his feet. He was such a coward. He'd already lost her, so how was this any better?

'I love you, Tilda and Matilda,' he said.

Too bloody late, buster.

Wasn't he always?

His pace increased to almost a jog as he zigzagged around pedestrians out for a stroll. No strolling for him. He was on a mission to quieten the noises in his head.

Tilda was shaking like she couldn't believe. Lachlan was avoiding her.

Sure, he had to go into work. It was part of being a surgeon to be called in even on days off, but today when they had issues to solve? Was she being a little selfish? Of course he had to go in. But at the moment it felt as though he was using it as an excuse to avoid her, and she'd already lost everything. No, not quite. Her hand landed on her stomach.

'I am pregnant.' So she needed to be ultra-careful because she could lose the baby too. To lose this one would be the end of everything. She'd never dream of happy families again.

She stuffed more clothes into the drawer in the spare bedroom. Slammed it shut. Sank onto the edge of the bed. A big bed, not quite as large as the one she and Lachlan had spent so many hours making love in but big enough if he should change his mind and visit her during the night. But there'd be no more lovemaking. She was back to being single. And that had nothing to do with the divorce.

I can't stay here with Lachlan just down the hall. It would only add to her despair. She loved the man to the end of the earth and back. She believed he didn't mean to hurt her. But she had to stand tall and be accountable for herself. So she couldn't stay here. They'd always be tripping over each other or trying to avoid one another. It would be awkward at the very least.

Not to mention how she'd feel if Faye or John turned up. Or Meredith.

Grabbing a bag, she emptied the drawer she'd just filled. Then she packed some books and shoes and her toiletries. She was out of here.

Where to?

The taxi driver suggested a hotel near Western General when she asked if he knew of anywhere within walking distance of her work. 'It's clean and safe,' he promised.

He was right. The room was rather dark and small but it was clean, and it was her space for as long as she paid the daily rate.

After dumping her bags on the bed, she headed outside for a walk. Anything to distract her from thinking about Lachlan. Of course it didn't work. He was with her every step she took.

He couldn't see how he was such a kind, loving man. His family adored him. Likewise those three boys and Meredith. He had all it took to be the best husband and father ever, if only he could move on from his past. Not that she was doing so well at that either. She knew what it was like to have your dreams stomped all over.

So was she ready to give him another chance? To let him back in, even though he couldn't love her? Was that being strong? She wasn't so sure.

Lachlan picked up his phone and called Tilda.

'Hello.' Her voice was flat. Tired. Full of tears.

'Where are you?' It was after eight and he'd just got home to find her gone. When had she left? After dealing with the patient he'd been called in to see and going for a walk, he'd been called back in to operate on another woman, an emergency this time, requiring a lot of work repairing face and chest injuries after being in a multiple car crash. He was exhausted but he knew sleep would be impossible until he was sure Tilda was all right.

'I've moved out of your place. It's too hard being there at the moment.'

'Where are you?' he repeated. He needed to know she was safe. Damn it, he needed to *see* her. To talk with her. Hug her. Like that was going to happen.

'I'm fine. Promise.'

Relief wasn't flooding him. 'Come back, Tilda. I won't even talk to you if you don't want me to.'

'No, Lachlan. I can't. You're the greatest guy I've known but I can't carry on staying with you. I need to get on with my own life. I have to look out for myself.'

The last shred of hope that she loved him died. But he still tried. 'I want to be there for you and the baby.'

'It's not enough, Lachlan.' She paused. 'Anyway, what happens when your family or Meredith turn up? I cannot look them in the eye and carry on acting as though I'm your fiancée.'

'I'll tell them the truth about that.'

'You need to. We were out of order doing it in the first place. But explaining it doesn't make the situation any better. We're a messed-up pair of individuals who need to sort our lives out, and the sooner the better for our baby's sake.'

'Tell me where you are, Tilda. I'm coming to get you. Please don't say no. We need to have this conversation face to face.'

'Sorry, Lachlan. It's too late for that. I am not coming back. Ever.' She was gone.

Not coming back, ever? Really? That was what she'd said. Did she mean it? It sounded like it.

He dropped onto a chair and stared up at the ceiling.

He loved her.

Which meant he had to risk it all and take a

chance on getting hurt again and let her into his heart for all to see. Not keep his love silent.

He could do that. The question was, did she want to hear it?

He picked up his phone, stabbed her number and listened to it ring and ring until the voicemail picked up. He couldn't tell her he loved her in a message.

So instead he simply said, 'I'll always be here for you, Tilda.' Then he went to bed, lying on her side and breathing in her scent from the pillow she slept with curled around her neck. He didn't get any sleep at all.

I'll always be here for you, Tilda.

She played the message over and over throughout the night, listening to every nuance in his voice, imagining him beside her. If only that was true. Except that would mean she'd gone back on her word to herself—to stay strong. She had to fight her own battles, not rely on Lachlan to be there for her. Not rely on anybody but herself.

It was too much. Throwing the phone aside, she climbed off the bed and dug out some fresh clothes. She'd go and find some breakfast then figure out what to do for the rest of the day.

Breakfast was a fail. It didn't stay down and she returned to her room to lie on her bed until the churning subsided. Then she looked up properties to rent and made three appointments for viewings. Even on Sundays some agents were hungry to make deals. To kill time she walked to Granville Island and had a coffee in the sun before heading to her first appointment.

The apartment was small and smelt of cats.

'No, thanks.'

The next one was clean and spacious and overlooked a nightclub.

'No, thanks.'

She didn't even bother looking at the third one. She was too tired, and couldn't keep Lachlan out of her thoughts.

She loved him.

But she was being strong and staying away.

It was so unbearably tempting to call a taxi and go back to his house. To tell him she loved him and beg him to try to put the past behind him and take a chance with her. That was not being strong.

She looked up jobs in other cities before sighing and switching her phone off. Avoidance was not the right tactic. She wouldn't keep father and child apart.

At eight o'clock she climbed into bed and pretended to sleep the night away. At least she'd be busy at work tomorrow and her mind would get a chance to quieten down.

As long as she didn't bump into Lachlan.

Only he was away at a day conference that she'd forgotten all about. Which made her feel lonelier than ever. She missed him so much every fibre in her body ached with the need to see him. This being strong wasn't going at all to plan.

Had she got it wrong? Would it make more sense to face up to her love and do something about seeing if they could make it work? If he could ever love her back? For their baby's sake, shouldn't she try?

Her heart thumped.

Could she?

The house was cold and quiet when Lachlan got home, dashing the small hope that Tilda might've returned. Throughout the day, when he was supposed to be listening to speakers talking about the latest in breast reduction procedures and scar repairs, he'd heard nothing other than Tilda saying she wasn't ever coming back to him.

Leaving his laptop on the bench, he headed upstairs for a shower, taking a detour to the spare bedrooms to check in case she had returned and was lying low. In the second room he looked in he found a small pile of books she'd left on the bedside table, but no clothes or make-up or shoes.

Spinning around to head for that shower, he saw a packet on the floor half under the bed. Bending down, he picked it up. A photo fell out onto the bedcover. A young Tilda was standing with an older woman, smiling as if her world was perfect.

He sank down onto the bed, unable to take his eyes off the two women. The likeness was incredible. The woman had to be Tilda's grandmother. They had the same twinkly eyes, identical smiles, and while Tilda's hair was dark and the other woman's grey, they both wore it in a ponytail that fell over their left shoulder. Two beautiful women. Two very strong women. One had no doubt passed that trait onto the other.

Shaking the packet, another photo slid out. In this one Tilda was holding up her nursing certificate and her grandmother was hugging her. The love in both faces touched him deeply.

'You were loved so much.'

'Yes, I was.'

His head shot up.

There she was, standing in the doorway, apprehension warring with determination in her beautiful face.

His heart began pounding, hard and fast. 'You dropped these.'

'I hoped they were here. I left in a bit of a hurry.'

'I can see where you get your strength from. Your grandmother was quite special, wasn't she?'

'She was, and she still is in here.' Her hand tapped her breast. 'I wish she was here now to know about the baby. About…' She paused, swallowed and locked her beautiful but sad eyes on him. 'I'm not as strong as I thought I was, Lachlan.'

He stood up and faced her. 'Yes, you are.'

'No. If I was, I'd have understood before now that being strong means showing my weaknesses to you. All of them.'

The pounding got louder and his mouth dried. 'That's not necessary.'

She stepped nearer, still watching him, as if she was begging him to see into her, to understand her. 'I thought I was being strong by standing alone, looking out for myself and ignoring what my heart wanted and needed.'

His pulse went into overdrive. Something momentous was coming. Good? Or terrible?

'I was wrong. It's hard for me to say this, but I need to. For me, for you, and for our baby.' Her shoulders rose and fell. 'I love you with all my being, Lachlan. I believe in you, trust you not to hurt me. I want to spend the rest of my life with you. If you'll have me,' she whispered. 'I don't want to raise our child alone. I want to show you how much I love you every day. And I want you to love me in return.'

He went to speak but nothing came out. Tilda loved him. He'd been longing to hear those words but hadn't expected to. If his tongue wasn't functioning his arms were; snatching her to him, he brushed the tenderest of kisses on her cheek, then her forehead and finally her lips.

'You're not taking all the blame for what's gone wrong between us. I was afraid to tell you I love you so much that my heart actually hurts, but the old fears wouldn't go away and then I thought I was too late anyway.' His heart was quietening, relaxing as the enormity of what Tilda had said finally sunk in. 'I should've been less of a coward and told you earlier anyway.'

'Are you still worried about losing someone again?'

'Yes, but I'm ready to take the chance and make the most of the time we've got together. I don't know about you, but I'm planning on for ever.'

Her lips lifted at the corners, making his heart melt all over again. 'I can't believe we were both madly in love with each other and neither one of us was brave enough to confess. I know we were both trying to protect ourselves, but we were going the wrong way about it. It nearly ended in disaster.'

'From now on, no more secrets.' He couldn't imagine not telling her he loved her every day from now on.

'Agreed.' Her mouth returned his kiss before she pulled back and eyeballed him. 'So? Are we going to spend the rest of our lives together? For ever?'

'Try and stop me.' He beamed. 'Yes, Tilda we are.' Taking her hands in his, he dropped to one knee. 'Will you make our engagement real? Marry me?'

Leaning down, she kissed him. 'Yes, Lachlan, I will.'

Then she was in his arms and they were kissing as if their lives depended on it. Which they did really. Without Tilda his life would be a cold, sad, barren wasteland.

As he laid her on the bed she looked up at him and laughed. 'Guess this means I'll have to let your mother organise our wedding and talk to that dressmaker.'

'Fine, but I'm the one taking you shopping

for an engagement ring.' If there was even
one out there that he'd consider being good
enough for her.

EPILOGUE

'LACHLAN, WHEN CAN Vicki play soccer with me?'

'Not for a couple of years at least, Lenny.'

'That's not fair. I want her to play with me now.' Stamp, stamp went his feet on the lawn at the back of their house. Meredith had dropped them off so she could spend the day with her new man, who was turning out to be a dream come true for her. Everyone was waiting with bated breath to see where this relationship went. Something that had Tilda laughing because it was a rerun of Lachlan's life before she'd arrived in it.

Tilda looked at Lenny. 'She's only a baby. Babies can't walk or run, and the ball is too big for her to hold.' The boys had taken to Vicki like frogs to water. They adored her but got impatient at times with her lack of activity. Gurgling and slopping milk out the corner of her mouth didn't cut it with them.

Grandma Faye handed Vicki to Tilda, nothing but love in her eyes. 'Think she needs the one thing I can't provide.'

Vicki's little face was screwed up in concentration, obviously about to tell everyone she wanted milk—now.

Latching her daughter onto her breast, trying to be discreet when the boys did their yuk faces, she leaned back against Lachlan's knees and smiled at the wonder of her world. Little more than a year ago she'd walked out into the arrivals hall at Phnom Penh Airport and up to the man holding a piece of card with Matilda Simmons written on it. Now she was Matilda McRae, though no one called her Matilda around here. She was strictly Tilda. And she was a mother to this gorgeous bundle of joy named after the woman who'd shown her how to be strong enough to let Lachlan into her heart. Her grandmother, Victoria.

'Want me to make some tea?' Faye was getting to her feet. At times the woman smothered her daughter-in-law with love, but she meant well and, along with John, was so happy for Lachlan. And therefore Tilda was more than happy to be spoilt.

'Not for me, Mum. I'd better be the sub for Vicki in the soccer game or there'll be bedlam on the pitch.' Lachlan had put up a goal net at each end of the lawn for the boys, admitting on the side that he'd only made his weekend mornings busier because they were determined to play there all the time. 'The ref's out of control.'

Tilda grinned up at him. 'John's loving every minute of it. And they're keeping you fit.'

Glancing around to see where his mother was, he then leaned down and whispered, 'You do that all on your own, Mrs McRae.'

Her heart sped up at the memory of what they'd got up to in their bedroom when Vicki had finally fallen asleep last night. 'Think you had something to do with it, Doctor.'

'Might've added my two cents' worth.'

'Cheap at the price, if you ask me. I might need to go a bit more upmarket.'

'A dollar?' He grinned. 'Love you, Tilda McRae. Vicki's one lucky little girl to have you for a mum.'

Her heart stuttered. She had taken to motherhood without hesitation. She'd been surprised at how natural it all seemed when she'd grown up with no one to observe. Of course Faye had been on hand from the moment she'd managed to sneak into the delivery room and meet her granddaughter for the first time but, to be fair, she didn't try and take over, merely acted as a guide if Tilda had any questions or doubts.

'Her dad's not too bad either.' In a lot of ways, not all to do with raising his daughter.

'Lachlan, hurry up,' Campbell shouted from the left goal net. 'We're waiting.'

'There's my cue.' He bent down again and brushed the softest and sexiest kiss over her mouth, then touched his daughter's back lightly. 'Love you both.'

'Love you too,' Tilda managed to say through the tears at the back of her throat. 'To the end of the earth and back.'

* * * * *

*If you enjoyed this story, check
out these other great reads from
Sue MacKay*

Brought Together by a Pup
Single Mom's New Year Wish
Stranded with the Paramedic
Fling with Her Long-Lost Surgeon

All available now!